A Triptych

Published by

NIYOGI
BOOKS

D-78, Okhla Industrial Area, Phase-I
New Delhi-110020, INDIA

Tel: 91-11-26816301, 26813350, 51, 52
Fax: 91-11-26810483, 26813830

email: niyogibooks@gmail.com
www.niyogibooks.com

Cover Design: Navidita Thapa
ISBN: 978-81-89738-39-6
Year of Publication: 2009

Printed at: Niyogi Offset Pvt. Ltd., New Delhi, India

A Triptych

THE SCAVENGER AND THE PAINTER

THE MAN WHO SAW COLOURS

THE PASSAGE OF SHADOWS

Dipanjan Rai Chaudhuri

NIYOGI
BOOKS

This book is dedicated to my friend
Subhas Ranjan Chakraborty,
who, among other things,
insisted that I put it into print.

Contents

THE SCAVENGER
AND
THE PAINTER

He entered the foyer. The welcoming faces before him dissolved into a blur as his eyes fell on the picture on the far wall. He walked in a trance towards it. It was, as he had thought, one of her masks. The scent of mimosa, which she liked to wear, assailed his senses even though there were no flowers in the foyer. Her laughter rang through the virtual portals of memory as a lump rose in his throat and moisture suddenly blinded the day.

THE SCAVENGER

I know how to wait; to wait and to watch. I have seen many a greenhorn salivating at the first sight of new, shining galvanised iron pipes on the terrace beyond the roadside wall right across my spot. I have seen them trying to unscrew and wrench away sections on summer nights, creating so much noise and commotion that the caretaker was forced to leave his bed to shoo them away.

I waited all monsoon before making a move, at times watching the rain pour down the pipes. On such days, I had to be content with retiring to the doorsteps of the haunted house with the overhanging balcony because once the street was flooded, my spot in the derelict shelter for bus passengers got swamped easily. But even more satisfying was the insidious trickle of the water, day after day, night after night, down the glistening pipes in a continuous stream. I could almost visualise the dark rust forming crusts inside the tiny crevices, eroding the once smooth surfaces into uneven cavities. When the sky cleared up, it was apparent that the shine had gone from the pipes. Invisible was the damage wreaked under the surface, where the wind and water had penetrated to eat up vital strength, especially in the section below the last joint.

I still waited, making do with powder or leaf, bought from the smaller vendors out of the proceeds of begging. These were augmented from time to time by some judicious snatching from cars at the traffic lights. If a woman was seated near the door with the window pane rolled down, I would whine in my most repellent manner and push my hand in, demanding alms. On my lucky day, a purse would be lying on the woman's lap. Nauseated or bored, the moment she would turn her head away from me, I would pull the purse out and dart back into the safety of the dark recesses between consecutive shops. Mostly, the woman would be too engrossed in coquetry or chatting, depending on the sex of her companion, and wouldn't notice what had happened till the car had moved through the crossing. Once or twice, a hue and cry had been raised, a pandemonium, but by then I had safely disappeared.

Other regulars of the street like the one-legged tea vendor saw everything, but I was safe, for there is a certain fellowship amongst those who live off the streets. He laughed vacuously after the victims had sped away, and then praised my dexterity and swiftness.

However, such opportunities were few, which was all the better, because regular snatching at the crossings would certainly bring in a relentless police hot in pursuit.

When the air turned nippy, I began to keep an overnight vigil over the pipes to ward off any stray punter who might have similar ideas. And finally, when the mornings became cold enough to deter anyone from leaving a cosy bed to investigate nightly noises, I decided to take action. My only problem was the old hag who lived on the ground floor of the house behind the shelter, on my side of the street. She never slept before the wee hours of the morning, pottering about her canvases, adding a daub of paint here, making a brush stroke there, her restless shadow reflected on the half-drawn curtains. Had she retired to bed at her usual hour however, I would still have had ample time to do my job before the first passengers from the suburban trains appeared in the alley which was a shortcut from the railway station to the street and beyond. The problem was that sometimes she stayed awake the entire night with the lights of her room switched on.

I finally zeroed in on a moonless night, and the night before, retrieved my tools from where I had stashed them after bringing them out from the haunted house. They were under a box in the tea-vendor's pavement stall. Thankfully, even the old hag went to bed at her usual hour, and I scaled the wall opposite, with a hammer, pliers and a towel-cloth in a bag hanging from my neck. Each step I took reminded me of my regular patrons who had cleared their conscience by handing out alms to me in my grimy and tattered half pants and T-shirt, as, mouth drooling, I mumbled incomprehensible words of praise or imprecation. They would hardly have recognised the smart cat-burglar sitting astride the wall and dropping soundlessly onto the other side. I thought of my compatriots from the street, and the local policemen who would also have been taken aback at my swift transformation.

Quite early in my career on the streets, I had realised that a physically weak, diminutive person like me could only survive if competitors, and there was no dearth of these in any locality of the metropolis, could be staved off by either fear or repugnance. I used both skillfully in my pretence of a lunatic and a scavenger. For the same reason, I never washed my clothes. Dirt caked in, making them stiff and a sooty black. At first, the smell disturbed me, but slowly it became less and less bothersome till it completely vanished from my conscious mind. My hair was matted and a muddy red. For a long time, when lice had bred in them, I had been troubled by their bites but now they had all died out, finding no place to hide among the solid sheets. Facial hair was sparse and apart from the stray louse or two, I had no problems there. I never pared my nails, unless forced to for reasons of convenience. They were hard and talon-like. In addition to this, I had taken to muttering obscenities, which initially was a conscious effort, but now came freely as a reflex.

However, before I had learnt the art of attire and attitude, I'd had a hard time on the streets, where every bit of space is apportioned and every bit of territory defended tooth and nail. So while prime spots offered shelter and some kind of privacy, I had to make do with the worst spots, in full public view. Even then, these spots could be used only for a short time because shopkeepers wanted clear pavements for their customers. Besides, the police would catch hold of newcomers first whenever they had quotas to fill. Even the worst spots were under the protection of some local lord of the street, though he might not have actually been using it.

On my first night on the city streets, I lay down beside a mound of sand on a pavement at what was one of the city's busiest junctions, something I discovered the very next morning. It was a particularly cold winter and I was misled by the deserted look of the crossroads at night. I was dropping from fatigue and hopelessness when I saw on the opposite pavement a group of workmen who had lit a fire from odds and ends, and were chatting noisily over their meal of gram paste and green chillies. They had thrown scraps of rubber and painted metal into the fire. To me, even the acrid, poisonous fumes seemed to reek of a haven of warmth and fullness. I was wrapped in the blanket I had been allowed to take from the last institution which threw me out for repeated thieving. All that now seem an eternity ago. The blanket was in tatters, just like the fragments of memory, and before long, shivering made sleep impossible on the stones of the pavement. I crossed the road and first squatted, and then lay down on the ashes of the workmen's fire. It was not really warm but not stony cold either and I fell asleep immediately till a hint of morning light woke up the stray dogs and drew them to my foreign smell. They were barking incessantly and with people stirring all about me, I gathered myself up quickly.

As the day brightened, I was overcome by sudden fright. Crossing the road, I cowered against the cold sand under the steady glare of the local goons as they sized me up. It was much later that I came to know they were doing this to estimate my worth in their fief, and to test my tenacity. I shrank under their scrutiny. Suddenly, there was a shrill cry and what I thought was an animal flew at my throat. As I shook it off, I saw that it was a human being, though man or woman, I still don't know, its incisors and nails displayed in classic animal aggression, bloodshot eyes brimming with hatred to horrify me into flight. I would have done exactly that had I been less frightened.

My hesitation threw the apparition into a kind of frenzy and, frothing at the mouth, it tried to claw my face, all the while spitting expletives. It was much smaller and weaker than I was, but I finally fled. This incident, in particular, was responsible for deciding in which avatar I should be seen in the city. I had understood well the strength which lay in the mind's horror of madness, and knew at once that I would use it as the perfect foil to the puniness of my frame.

Getting picked up or arrested generates mixed feelings. Food and shelter is free and assured, but the police are rough handlers and hit hard in the worst of places. When I was younger, the inevitable sodomy in prison was an added cross to bear. Now, of course, I was well-known and the police would not lend a hand in giving me free boarding and shelter. In the two weeks, when the wind, whistling along the empty streets, is cold enough to awaken the aches and pains in most bones, or the month when rains pour down every day and gutters regularly spill over, leaving dark, evil-smelling residue all over the pavement, the prison is an excellent home for an old habituated convict like me.

That night, the sky was clear and the stars shone like jewels. Fortunately, to help me, there was a biting wind and I worked, secure in the knowledge that no one would even think of peeping out of a window, let alone stir out to investigate the unavoidable little noises accompanying any work with metal.

The caretaker I knew would be snugly ensconced in bed with the local prostitute who walked the alleyways of the area, providing comfort and disease to expatriates like him from distant villages, far from wife and home.

Did I feel the cold? Fortified with the powder, I never felt the weather. However, I had with me another blanket stolen from the old hag one autumn afternoon, from a pile set out for airing. This I draped about myself when I settled into bed. Two bouts of pneumonia had taught me that the powder was a deceiver which sharpened some faculties, but dulled most senses. I was safe as long as I was active, but cold is on the lookout for passivity and gets to you fast once the resting body drops its defences.

The last section of the pipe came apart easily in my hands without alerting anyone, and I hid it quickly. I knew that if a policeman caught sight of it, he would sell it himself. Not only would he give me nothing, he might think it safer to kick me away from his beat altogether.

The hour before dawn is the best time for such risky transactions and the section was lost in the scrap-dealer's yard long before the sharp-eyed health freak from the first floor of the house saw the mutilated end of the pipe. He raved and ranted till a reluctant caretaker materialised to shout back that the wages would have to be increased twofold if they expected him to double up as a night watchman too. Other windows opened and in the general confusion that followed, I slinked away.

The local policemen strolled in towards the evening. The second officer was corrupt to the core, but he was aware of everything that went on in the neighbourhood. He was shrewd enough to have a fair idea of what had happened and came to stand above me, beside my spot. Then he prodded me with a baton borrowed from a constable while I cowered in a foetal position and mumbled and cackled, putting up one of my best shows of mindlessness.

He laughed, 'I shall personally beat you black and blue if this is repeated in this house, you monkey! Don't try to deceive me with your play-acting.' I know he had said that half-heartedly because nobody in the burgled house had even offered him tea. He knew them to be a stingy lot and also knew that the pipes were common property and no occupant would singularly take the trouble of pursuing the police with speed money. So did I, and I also understood the psychology of people and took only such things and such quantities which would not hurt enough to make anybody pursue the chase. As it was, storm water would spread in the passageway to some extent because the end of the pipe was lost, but nobody would be seriously affected by this.

The second officer gave me another prod in the ribs and moved on.

Sections from pipes were good merchandise and fetched the price of more than a month's powder. When I managed to lay hold of a good counter like a pipe-end, I usually bartered powder for ampoules.

In another hiding place in the haunted house, I kept my syringe and needles. Time was, when I had to fish them out from the bin where the local nursing home emptied its refuse in blatant contravention of the laws for the disposal of medical waste. The law, I know from jail, the great university from where I also learnt about hepatitis B and AIDS. Death, I can contemplate. But disease terrifies me as does old age. I have nightmares in which I lie, feeble and emaciated, stuck to my spot without the wherewithal for a shot or even a snort, flies settling on me and dogs sniffing away, waiting to catch the first whiff of the odour of death.

I am better organised now. Every week I go for a round of the shops in my territory to collect my fee. I am no parasite. The work I do to keep body and soul together, is a part and parcel of the method of waste processing developed spontaneously by the metropolis. As a scavenger, I deserve the fee I collect. Shopkeepers are well aware of this and hand me bags of rubbish to sift through before dumping them in the waste bin. In fact, I am almost a mascot for them. They are a superstitious lot and most of them fear bad luck if they chase me away. A few, on the other hand, take *me* for bad luck and their shops I have learnt to avoid.

One of the shops on my rounds is a drugstore. Around noon, when business slows down due to the siesta hour, the owner departs for lunch, and the assistant sometimes goes off for a minute or two to the public conveniences, signalling me to keep an eye on the shop's affairs. The shop owner also dispenses injections and keeps a heap of disposable syringes with needles in an open box, behind the counter. The moment the assistant disappears, I turn back and using my body as a shield to the streets, remove one set from the box. I make sure never to take more than one at a go.

All day, I nurse the ampoule in my bosom, anticipating and gloating over the bliss to follow. As the poison races through my blood, the pleasure slowly steals over and covers me in a sheath of ecstasy and finally peace. Having a woman is commonplace compared to the pleasures hidden in the needle.

All this clearly shows how good I am at waiting. For the old hag, I have been waiting for eight years now, ever since a police van dumped me at this intersection. At first I thought she lived alone and would be an easy prey. But then, I didn't know that she never left the flat and, forgetful as she was, never kept the box I coveted near a window. She never left her door unlocked. I learnt later that it was a precaution she took to protect her paintings. Tradesmen called on her and a washerman took out soiled clothes.

Judging by the departure of canvases in roll covers or crates, there was a small but steady sale of her stuff, though what people saw in them beats me. Windows, she left open all the time and in all seasons, and I peeked regularly at the most recent canvases in the afternoons, when she took a nap. In my opinion, there was no proportion and no perspective; moreover, the colours jarred and clashed. For sometime now, the sales had been taking a dip. However, after she began painting masks in black and white—so macabre that despite seeing them from a distance, they came to haunt me in nightmares and left me trembling and clutching myself—sales improved.

At first, there were regular get-togethers at her flat that lasted way into the night. Many of the visitors had to be rich if the automobiles they were using were really theirs. I saw well-dressed men and women circulating under bright lights among the canvases with long-stemmed glasses in their hands. There would be at least one exhibition a year when a well-dressed man, very serious and sober-looking, except for the indulgence of a luxuriant pair of moustaches, whom I dubbed the Agent, would come and carry away canvases in crates and bring back the unsold ones after a fortnight or so. An exhibition was usually followed by a string of midnight soirées. Some of the cars had stickers marked 'Press' on them.

The Agent never stayed the night but some others did. I wouldn't say she was promiscuous; these occasions were infrequent and usually occurred after I saw her finish a canvas. She would leave it on the easel and come back and look at it again and again. Sometimes on the third or fourth day she would tear it up. Otherwise, she would start putting finishing touches. After seven days, she would lose interest in it and take a man.

She was quite catholic in her taste. I have seen many types of men come and go, short and tall, fair and dark, unkempt and smart, gentleman and knave. But there was one rule till the recent events. However frequently the man might have been a guest of hers before staying the night, he was never admitted afterwards.

Usually they themselves never came back. But she did have trouble with the occasional admirer who was persistent, and I saw her shutting the door softly but firmly in the face of at least two of them.

One night, I woke up to the sound of car doors slamming. I opened my eyes just in time to see the Agent disappear through the doorway of the hag's flat. Shortly afterwards, an ambulance was parked in front of the shelter, lights blazing, and men with a stretcher went into the flat. They came out bearing the slight frame of the old hag. I took a quick peek at her face, my first in so many years. It was the face of a girl, almost belying the age suggested by her grey hair, the emaciated neck and hands knotted with blue veins. Her eyes were not relaxed as in sleep, but shut tight.

The moment they left, I saw my chance and slipped into the narrow, paved passage between the boundary wall and the building, but the Agent had been careful. No lights had been left on and all the windows were shut. I was excited by this event, feeling sure that my time was coming.

When she returned after two months, she was dragging a foot, and had to be helped into the flat by the Agent, but she continued with her earlier routine, except that she broke her rule regarding men. There were, however, no more parties, and no exhibitions either. The Agent came by faithfully as often as he did earlier, but he took out rolls or crates infrequently. The cars marked 'Press', which earlier were to be seen off and on parked in front of the bus shelter, disturbing me and violating traffic laws, were now rarely visible. I cackled to myself in glee on seeing the bird thus grounded, and waited patiently.

THE PAINTER

When I came to, I realised I was in a hospital. Nothing can match that synthetic neatness of the rooms or the deceptive reassurance of that sanctimonious odour. The next thing I understood was that I could not move either my right leg or arm. The world was, of course, a kind of a hazy blur, viewed without my glasses. I resisted a tug in my brain prompting me back to sleep and took stock of the damage wreaked on my body.

From what I understood, I would have to train my disobedient body to sit and stand and walk again with only half my muscles working. Sitting up was quite a feat, more so because I found that I was weak, and even a little exertion called for disproportionate effort. It took me ten minutes to sit up, and by the end of the exercise, I was panting and sweating. A nurse had materialised by that time and threatened to jab a sedative into me before I agreed to postpone my investigation into how much or how little I could push myself. She gave me my glasses and I came to know the worst. Even with them, the world was dark and obscure and all colours were muted.

I had been unconscious for the past ten days and my left limbs were quite stiff too. I insisted on meeting the physiotherapist without delay, and within two days, picked up a shuffling gait, dragging the right foot along as I moved. The right arm with its useless appendage of a hand, hung on the side. However, in the past couple of days, I had sufficiently penetrated the taciturnity of the therapist to learn that there was some life in my right leg, and he would be able to train me to use it fully. But a question regarding the right arm and hand only drew a blank.

Every day, he stood by watching while I tried hard to move this arm. My whole body convulsed to force some kind of a movement but failed. Even with intense, concentrated effort, all I could do was just twitch some muscles closer to the shoulder joint. Sweat beads formed on my face to join together and run down in thin streams, but the arm couldn't, wouldn't budge. The mirror reflected my flushed face with lines of effort and pain clearly etched over it. I tried again and again, but after a few attempts at movement, I had to lie down as my body shook convulsively. I was almost ready to give up. My therapist, however, thought otherwise. He would allow me to rest at this point, but when I had recovered sufficiently, would immediately ask me to start working on my fingers.

I tried to will motion into those inert members which had had almost a life of their own, flowing with the brush over the canvas and creating lines and juxtaposing colours almost without my knowledge of how they did it. I took over really after the main picture had emerged. Only the finishing touches were consciously mine. At that stage, I knew what I wanted and did it, but till then, the picture created itself, my hand possessed by it and with it. Now they lay stiff, as inert as parts of a corpse's arm, never again to know the exultation of creation. I was told that although results did not seem forthcoming at the moment, I was to continue my efforts to move the right arm and the right hand. Greater miracles had been reported.

Later in the day, I was taken on a wheelchair, to the eye department, where a doctor shook his head and wrote down a mixed placebo of nutrients and vitamins.

That evening when my faithful friend, who had brought me to the hospital, came to visit me with flowers and chocolates, I impressed upon him that I wanted to be discharged from the hospital.

Usually, I cajoled or blustered my way past his objections in various matters, but this time, he proved remarkably firm, rejecting outright any plan of returning alone to my flat. I was equally adamant in my opposition to an attendant in the flat. There were only two rooms, I argued. One I slept and worked in, the other stored my canvases. I needed the space for myself and, no doubt, the other person would also need some space. He had no idea how much space people needed. I finally told him that there was a strong possibility that within a week, either I would kill the attendant, or he/she would kill me. Perhaps he believed more in the possibility of the former happening, which is why he shut up for the rest of the day.

The next day however, he came to see me with a young man, about thirty or so in years, I assumed. I glowed under the admiration which leaped into his eyes as soon as he saw me. My friend introduced him as a lecturer in aesthetics, the son of a valued client, an ardent fan of my paintings; but what I could discern in his eyes was not admiration for my work but an appreciation of the woman herself. He was inviting me to stay in his house where one floor, where his parents lived, would be empty for three months as they had left on a long holiday. I would not be alone in the house which was why my friend had mooted the idea in the first place, but I would be undisturbed.

I relented. It had been a long time since I had inspired admiration of another kind in a man. My friend had chosen well, for the young blade added that his father had seen my work just before I had been struck by paralysis, and had expressed a desire to acquire the complete series.

Soon I was settled in a sunlit room with large French windows overlooking the beautifully landscaped garden. And even though I hadn't asked for them, there was an easel and paints and all the other paraphernalia essential to my painting, at hand. The young man it seemed, dabbled in painting too. I could not, much as I wanted to, encourage him because though his work which he brought out reluctantly and after much persuasion, showed an original flair for composition, he had no eye for line or proportion. He could not draw.

He understood what I was saying at once, in spite of my prevarications and a sharp pain stabbed me even as the light faded in his eyes, only to flash back when I gently touched his hand to say, 'Life is much more than the pictures we paint of it.'

He still had the resilience of youth and it was important that somebody told him the truth before he grew older. He concealed his disappointment, but only I knew how deep it must have been. It is a tragedy when one has the painter's eye but not the painter's hand. In my long career, I have seen many an amateur fall to the depths of despair. Later, I came to know how close to those depths he had been, and how it was only the sense that I was responding to his admiration, which had restrained his downfall.

In such a strange yet agreeable atmosphere, I began to teach my left hand to draw. It was difficult at first and I shared for a while the same predicament as that of my admirer, whose hand had also refused to be directed by his vision. Moreover, I could stand only with some support from an upright column. I chose a corner and placed the easel so that I could reach it from a half-slouch, with my back against a wall. The task was not made any easier by my general debility and a weakness in my good hand and leg, which told me how close I had come to losing control of all my limbs.

My hand tired easily at first, and I had to rest it frequently till my good leg began to shake under me, and I had to sit down on the floor. After a short rest, I would get up again, and this continued till I became light-headed and the world around me began to darken. Then I had to lie down quickly to bring back light to my damaged eyes. My peripheral vision told me that he always lingered in the adjoining room, watching over me, but he was both sensitive and sensible enough to understand that it was a battle I had to win alone. Nobody could help.

After about a week or so, I managed to coax some sort of obedience from my left hand, and turned my mind to colour. I had been facing some trouble with colours in my everyday activities, but the memory my mind retained of them helped and, as I later understood, prevented me from appreciating the full extent of my loss. When I tried to put colours on the canvas, they failed to make sense. It was worse when I tried to mix them. I called out to him and, when he came, asked him to describe the colour scheme I had put on the canvas. With a rueful air he responded that what he saw on the canvas was sheer nonsense.

The burden of failure was too heavy to bear.

I sat down.

Then my left hand and leg began to tremble uncontrollably. I couldn't still the shaking till I jammed them against the wall. I stared out of the window with unseeing eyes. The blue of the sky was a memory superimposed on what I actually saw now. I would never again know what colour the sky really was. I would never again know the riot of colours at sunset or follow the change in the hue of leaves and flowers as the light slowly brightened through the morning.

I had become my own blank canvas.

I don't know how long I had been sitting in front of that window. He finally came and took me in his arms. I collapsed against him in complete exhaustion. He gently lifted me off the floor and carried me to the bed. I began trembling again but when he held me close, the trembling stopped and the rigidity left my limbs. He let out a sigh. Then carefully, he undressed me as if I were a butterfly whose wings would tear if there was the slightest friction.

He was just as patient and careful in his lovemaking; holding and touching me as if I were a girl he was initiating into intimacy. His tenderness almost made me believe that I really was that girl, and not an experienced whore who is frightened of having lost a nerve too many to respond to arousal. But he was a patient lover, waiting, knowing that this first-time reassurance was more important than passion, and I touched the pinnacle of pleasure that calmed me down to a restful sleep.

After this, I could not live in his father's house. He couldn't see my point of view at first and was alternately contrite and insistent. But then he came around, unlike my faithful friend, who, I now understood, had thought of transferring me here for good. Of course, as expected he did not understand why I wanted to shift back to my own house, though he had a gnawing suspicion of what had taken place.

I came home to find everything arranged to suit me, easel and all. My darling had come the day before to do this. In the morning, two or three neighbours called to ask after my health, and, of course, my stalker was at his post as usual. I could no longer make out his face, but I had seen those eyes in their deep sunken sockets, staring, and the high, simian cheekbones so many times that what I could not see, I could well imagine.

He came in the evening, just as the sun was setting at the far end of the street. I was sitting at the window facing the street, fretting for him when he made his appearance like a spectre, silhouetted against the sky with the glow of the sunset behind him. As he walked towards me, my heart raced with joy and then slowed down and I suddenly saw the day when I would be sitting here, waiting, and he would not come. I was wondering whether he would stay the night, if what had happened in his studio had only been the effect of a particular time and place which could not be replicated elsewhere and at another time, when he took off his jacket, loosened his shirt and settled in my armchair, smiling at me all the time.

He left at dawn, and as I sat at the window, watching him disappear, a great sadness stole upon me because around the corner, death stood waiting for me. Extinction didn't scare me, but I did not want to leave this world where he would continue to live, his eyes smiling and his laughter rolling into the morning. My life, it seemed to me, had been a long wait for him. Now that I had found him, how could I let him go?

Every time he gazed into my eyes for long, the same despair welled out of them and made him restless, for I never told him the cause. How could I tell him about the refuge I had finally found in him? Of the yearning that I could not distance myself from? How could I tell him I was dying and didn't want to leave him? In desperation, I drew mask after mask, and each of these was a death mask. He looked at them often perplexed, hypnotised, yet not recognising the eye of death.

Then the day came. The street grew dark, but he didn't come. At first, I thought he must have been held up in traffic. After an hour of pacing the room, I tried to get myself to believe that he had some urgent work in his father's office. Suddenly, I realised that the room I was sitting in was completely dark, with the exception of the scanty light stealing past the curtains. I switched on all the lights. From each direction, the canvases stared at me. The hours crept by and my left limbs began to tremble as I finally faced the prospect that he might not come. I regretted, for the first time in my life, my obstinate stand against possessing a telephone. But why hadn't he told me that he might be held up? Something unexpected had happened. Was he dead? Lying forlorn in some mortuary? Or left spreadeagled on some road, surrounded by the omnipresent but passive onlookers of the city?

When the street began to quieten down, I left my post at the window and resumed my pacing. The thought flashed across my mind that he wouldn't come again. He had found someone nearer his age. I didn't will the thought; I'd much rather do without it. All my life I had faced what had come to me without worrying about the outcome. Now my will was failing me because I had never before found anything or anyone so precious and never had my grasp ever faltered so. I looked into the mirror and saw the enemy within me stare back. Every passing day, the enemy gained a day and I lost one.

This was how it must have ended, I thought. The nights he decided to stay away without informing me, I would even begin to imagine what she looked like and picture them laughing together, strolling with arms intertwined. Were they lovers yet? The thought would seize my chest in a vice-like grip and wouldn't let go till I drank myself into a stupor. Then he'd come in the morning and looking into his eyes, I'd forget the anguish of the night before. But he could read my thoughts and laughed at my predicament. I would rather die than ask him where he had been and what he had been doing. He, without being demonstrative, however, would weave the information of his whereabouts in ordinary talk to set my heart at rest. But the whore that I had been so long before I met him, I suffered again the same ache, the next time it happened.

THE SCAVENGER

She rejoiced on her return home, throwing open all windows and curtains with the alacrity of a new bride. After washing her face, she limped through the rooms again and again, touching things, holding them up before her eyes, making little changes in their arrangement while the Agent sat and went through the medley of bills which had accumulated since he had last come. Where she had kept the box in her absence, I could not figure out, but now it was out again, beckoning me like flashes from a lighthouse.

The Agent left and, to my immense delight, she lay down to rest though a little uncharacteristically. As I had anticipated, her flight would never be the same again. She got up when the shadows fell on her windows and, with a plate of snacks beside her, stood at the window looking down the road. It was as if she was having a panic attack. From the window, she would go back into the room, pace restlessly and come back to the window again. She switched on her music system and the strange mixture of harmony and discord, which she so preferred, swelled out onto the street. I disliked this music and, in any case, resented the intrusion into my auditory space. Usually, when she embarked on this trip, it lasted at least an hour, but this time she switched off the music suddenly and started her pacing up and down once more.

Finally, a young man, presentable and athletic, showed up at the far end of the road. She hurried inside as quickly as she could manage, the lame hag, and I understood. She had been waiting for her paramour. When the man entered the flat, I recognised him. He had come to the apartment the day before, but at that time I could not tell which flat he had visited. The sly fellow had not opened the windows of the flat then. She got on my nerves with her jittery behaviour. Every afternoon, the same drama was enacted. She would fret and fidget as she waited for him.

I had never seen her do anything like this in the course of her previous liaisons. In the morning, after he left, for he stayed most nights, she remained on a kind of high. She took to singing a tune I never could place, though it remained tantalisingly familiar. I call it a tune for want of a name. She was tone deaf and the shrill notes she produced grated on my senses. Yet the sequence was familiar. I supposed all this indicated joy. Then why did she, in its midst, take to staring at the sky?

Sitting at the window, her brow would suddenly furrow deep with contemplation. This happened most nights just before dawn. She wouldn't switch on a light, presumably to keep the paramour from waking up, but parted the curtains to peer out of the window.

I would see her from my shelter, face tilted skywards, the street lights making a strange chiaroscuro of it. She would sit like this, sleepless for hours, shifting her line of vision only when the occasional truck sped along the deserted street. I would drop off to sleep and wake up with a start time and again. She was disturbing my sleep too. When the crows began their raucous response to the paleness in the sky or when the muezzin started calling the faithful to their morning prayers, she would draw the curtains and retire to the inside, where, no doubt, the paramour would be sleeping the deep sleep of the young. But she wouldn't go back to bed. She would potter around in the kitchen, make tea for herself and breakfast for him. Then she would sit with the mug of tea behind the curtains till the man awoke.

Pretty soon, he would draw the curtains apart, wash up and then hurry through the breakfast, leaving the flat even before the caretaker of the house stirred.

As he would step out on the street, he would turn and wave and she would stand at the window gazing into the distance, long after he would disappear.

She would then start work on the canvases. But there was a difference; where earlier she worked through the whole morning even after a party night, now she got tired within an hour or so, and slept till noon.

Whenever he didn't turn up in the evening, she wouldn't sleep the night through, pacing up and down the room, her shadow falling on the curtains and disappearing again, till it became a torture for me to watch and wait for the shadow to appear again, just as the ears strain to hear the next drop from a leaking tap to patter onto the basin below.

She always drank in the evenings, and on these occasions, the session would continue late into the night. By morning, exhausted she would collapse on her bed and doze off till noon.

Once, he was absent for five days. From the morning of the third day, she began to drink till she dropped. She didn't glance at her canvases even once! But the moment he appeared, she was her noisy self again, her laughter assailing my ears whenever I tried to relax in my shelter. Every time he played truant, I hoped he had tired of her. But he always came back. What *did* he see in her, the besotted fool? All the while, she went on drawing those terrible masks. They became even more grotesque when within a few days of her return, she began to paint in black and white. She made a pitiful figure at the easel, with her right arm hanging down rigid and lifeless. I couldn't help stifle a chuckle when, suddenly at times, an awkward movement of her body, would set the arm swinging. She was a sight; trying to stop the swinging with her left hand and desperately contorting her body to keep her balance on one leg.

She rarely had any visitors now apart from the faithful Agent. The gigolo had swallowed her up. When he came, but did not stay the night, she slept better, and I could look in. The box remained on her bedside table, out of my reach. Every time I looked in, I tried the door, hoping she would have made the mistake, and I wanted to make sure that on the day the mistake was made, I would be there to make the most of it.

My vigil was rewarded within the year.

The paramour had not stayed the night. Awakened by the cold, I glanced at the flat and almost jumped up. A sliver of light framed the door to the flat. I could hardly believe my eyes! Slowly, I shed my cocoon of a covering and crouched up nearer to the house. The thoroughfare was deserted; the street lights orange, like solitary eyes, stared through the fog. It was the hour when even stray dogs take a shut-eye. I felt the warmth of expectation coursing through my body and straightened up. Crossing the road and tiptoeing over to the open window, I peeped in through chinks in the hastily drawn curtains.

She lay on the carpet with arms and head down on the shallow bed. I looked for long at the body. It was quite still. There were no signs of life.

The sky was still dark with the night and there were no stars. The cold was forbidding and the street remained deserted, enveloped in fog. Crab-like, I sidled towards the door of the flat. After looking out, when I was certain that there were no observers, I squeezed into the narrow gap through which light seeped out like body fluid.

The door opened into a narrow passage with the washroom on the right, doors slightly ajar, lights on, vomit all over the tiled floor. On the left was the door to her room where she lay sprawled half on the floor and half on the bed. She had been trying to reach the bed when she fell. I waited at the door for a while but caution was not required.

Her flight was over.

The box was on the bedside table. It was made of silver with the most delicate and exquisite filigree work. The lid was curved and beside the keyhole was a tiny button which, no doubt, operated the catch securing the lid. I had been fantasising for long about how to deal with the box. It was not small enough to be hidden in my clothes. But, again, it was not so delicate that the lid could be pried open noiselessly, if at all. In my fantasy, however, I had always visualised my entry into the flat when it was empty. I had never expected the end to be like this, where her lifeless body would be lying at my feet.

If she carried the key on her person, I reflected, my problem would be solved and there would be no question of searching through her belongings. Otherwise, I would be in for a prolonged hunt through the disorder of her rooms, fraught with the danger of being discovered. That however, did not make me shrink from searching the body. It was nothing but a hunk of meat now, food for maggots and the unseen hosts of bacteria who always, in the end, proved stronger than humans. They were the ultimate scavengers who, with their efficacy and strength, had taught me humility and showed me my lowly place in the hierarchy of the scavengers' pyramid. I pressed the button beside the keyhole, expecting it to be unyielding and almost gasped with surprise when the button gave in and the lid lifted slightly. The catch had come undone. Her carelessness had persisted to the end and she had not locked the box after all. I lifted the lid, my hands trembling with excitement and elation. I had been waiting for this moment for the past eight years …

Reality never lives up to expectations. It was a lesson life had been trying to teach me all along, but one which I had obviously not learnt. Otherwise, why was I disappointed? The box was not empty. There was one small, translucent, creamy-white sphere resting in a depression in a square of deep-blue velvet. It was a pearl, no doubt, but only one and a small one at that. There was nothing else.

I looked with hatred at the body. Why had she clung to this box with its meagre content with all the pretence of guarding a treasure? It was her attitude which had bred and fed my longing for years, till it had become almost the *raison d'être* for my life, my Holy Grail. 'Despicable b-------,' I cursed her roundedly, to be huddling over the remnant of some lechery which she must have sentimentalised into some sort of an idyllic dream.

Of course, I took the pearl. It was better than nothing.

The easels in this front room were empty. Brushes, and tubes of paint littered the floor. Half a bottle of scotch and a tumbler with about two fingers of whisky stood on a bedside table. A diary lay open on this table with an uncapped pen between the open sheets. The cap had dropped to the floor. The room was extremely untidy, with clothes strewn all over. A black panty and brassiere set lay crumpled in one corner. The floral design in white thread bore testimony to the vanity and infatuation which had forgotten age and seemliness. Books were scattered here and there on the ground. On a coffee table lay half a cup of tea, with torn skin floating on the murky liquid, and the day's newspaper. The morning would bring in the flies.

I moved into the inner room. Canvases were stacked in sheets and rolls. A few laminated canvases stood against the walls. The windows were all shut and the room was filled with the still acrid smell of paint. This room had only a night light on. I switched on the main lights—tube lights on two walls and a globe hanging from the centre of the ceiling. The globe was actually an outer cover of a bulb and dead moths had crowded together in a black heap at its centre.

Three easels stood on the floor carrying canvases with preliminary sketches in pencil. They were all sketches of masks. Through the repelling individuality of each mask, something familiar seemed to reach out to me.

I crept closer for better scrutiny.

Staring at the sketches, a horrible suspicion began to take shape in my mind. I ran to the finished canvases and looked closely at the images. They too were masks, and a terrible realisation dawned on me, even before I hastily shut my mouth. It was my face in all the drawings—distorted, grotesque and hateful!

I rushed into the front room in anger, kicked the body and watched it roll onto the floor. I seized a palette knife from a shelf and going back to the other room, tore the canvases to ribbons. I was contemplating mayhem on the other stacks and rolls too, but the loudspeaker at the mosque blared into life at that very moment almost telling me that my time had run out. I hurried out with the pearl, stopping only to gnash my teeth at the body. I gained my shelter without incident. Nobody was up yet. It was too cold. I realised now why the masks had given me nightmares.

I had underestimated her malevolence. While I had been watching her, she too had been weaving her evil design. How many masks she had sent into the world already, I didn't know.

Now that business was dull, hopefully, the canvases in the back room would go to the dustbin or, at least, rot in oblivion in some dark corner of the Agent's storeroom.

THE MAN WHO SAW COLOURS

THE FIRST ENCOUNTER

She was a city girl. Her earliest memory was of the ubiquitous and haphazardly placed television antennae, seen through a window grill, against a lumpy mass of cloud so white that the glare almost hurt her eyes. It must have been the end of the rains; a time just before the feathery autumn clouds invaded the clear blue sky.

Like all city people, she had a love–hate relationship with it. Therefore, this morning, she had expected the metropolis to relinquish its hold over the scene only very gradually, but the bus route rode right across the industrial suburbs in a shortcut and soon the landscape, sliding past her window, became monotonously flat. There were lush green paddy fields on both sides of the highway, bound into a grid by raised mounds of earth, continuously crisscrossing through the gaps between gnarled old trees. The monotony of the flat grid was such that even the dusty, noisy crossroads and marketplaces, with their share of the local populace, were a relief.

Fellow travellers and people on the road, could easily sense an aura of the metropolis about her, casting furtive glances or, quite often, blankly staring at her. She was dressed casually in jeans and a simple top, an attire still not common in these parts, but to her surprise, not entirely absent either. Among the young girls boarding the bus in groups of twos and threes, students from a degree college further down the road as she could make out from their chatter, she could see signs of a dress sense similar to that of the city. And even though she wore no make-up and her long, black hair had been braided conservatively, the awkward glances of the people on the road and in the bus were for her and her alone. This unwarranted attention irked her a bit.

The country, too, wasn't what she'd believed it to be. Right next to her, she was surprised to overhear two women discussing their jobs in a post office and a bank, things which had been exclusive to the big city so far. And here, on the outskirts of the countryside, their white-collar jobs invited not a single comment nor were the incumbents awarded even a second glance!

Her cousins were sitting apart at windows behind her and she craned her neck to find them sleeping tight like new-born babies. They were both much older, her father having been the youngest of five brothers and three sisters—all of whom were dead now. Her six other cousins, also coming in like her to the ancestral village today, worked and lived in suburban satellite cities of the ever-expanding metropolis. These two whom she had accompanied, were brothers and lived about an hour away from the tiny one-storeyed apartment where she lived with her mother.

She had once been a toddler swaying unsteadily around their legs while they were adolescents, because their fathers had shared accommodation for a few years, between two spells of infighting and splitting. Their parents' generation had been a quarrelsome one, and it was only after they had all passed away that it had become possible for all concerned to sit together over the jointly shared ancestral lands.

The two brothers had watched her grow into a lovely and accomplished young woman and though they still found it difficult to come to terms with her transformation, they were extremely protective of her whenever they all went out together.

As the bus emptied its load of people commuting to work or school, it picked up passengers of another kind—people who were on a shorter trip and were talking animatedly of the rains or the lack of them, fluctuations in the market prices of vegetables, the iniquity of cold-storage owners and the arrogant, self-assertive behaviour of hired labour.

No one sat beside her.

The odd woman or two who did board the bus, their clothes reeking of the world of hired labour, preferred cowering at the front of the bus. She would later learn from her rural cousins that thirty years ago, such women used to sit on the floor of the bus and wouldn't even dare to rest their backs on the seats!

The day was turning sultry and she too began to doze off in the wet claustrophobic heat. This wasn't good for her because, while she stayed awake, her attention was engaged in absorbing new impressions from around her. However, even a short nap, relaxed her self-control enough to allow the events of the morning to rerun in her mind in a flash of distaste. She not only saw herself drawing the bedclothes up to her neck, looking at her friend at the bedroom door but could distinctly feel his touch, and the reluctance of her body, and was jolted to a palpitating wakefulness by it. Her friend lived next door. His family had been there for three generations. His father had become friends with the ill-tempered man who'd spent all his savings building a house for his wife and daughter. Hence the two children, the boy a year younger than the girl, grew up together, romping about in both houses. Her mother, being a school teacher, ran short of time for much neighbourliness, but the boy's mother, affectionate and easy-going of nature, more than made up for the lack; especially after the death of the girl's father. This event brought the boy's father to extend a sort of guardianship over her, and he perhaps knew more of what went on inside the head of the quiet girl than her own mother.

What none of the parents knew of, was that from an almost academic exploration of each other's little bodies, they had reached a level where they had discovered the pleasures of touching and climaxing even before they heard and read the usual insinuations about it through their peers and seniors. As a result, they indulged themselves clinically and without any guilt, until the boy began to develop a strong possessiveness. This was perhaps his way of falling in love, while she remained emotionally detached, despite a deep affection for him. Over a period of time, there was a genuine concern over his indolence, which was fast becoming the hallmark of how spoilt he was. Their physical explorations however, remained unimpeded and went unnoticed by their unsuspecting parents who acknowledged their need for privacy as a part of growing up.

As she grew into a young woman of some beauty and intellect, earning excellent grades and showing a flair for creative writing, she was praised and wooed and greatly fussed over by boys and young men, to the intense chagrin of her friend. His insecurity was reflected in his fierce need of being extremely aggressive with her, especially when he forced on her attentions which he imagined to be giving her pleasure. The fact of the matter though was, that, to her, the intimacy became more and more a violation as she matured and it began to dawn on her that love was something which she definitely did not feel for the young man.

After every incident like this morning's, she decided to terminate the relationship, but never succeeded in taking the final plunge. This was not because of the tiny flicker of involuntary, clinical pleasure which she unwittingly betrayed, at times, to his elation, but because she knew and was afraid he would fly into an all-consuming rage. It wasn't as if she hadn't tried. Once she had resisted him for six months. However, her genuine concern for him had worn her down, when his sleeplessness and loss of appetite not only shook up his parents, but worsened to fever and a persistent cough. Finally, he had to be taken away to the hills among his mother's people, to be treated for suspected consumption.

The sun was directly overhead, when they arrived and shadows were minimal. Overnight bags were all they had as luggage, and because, as usual, there were no conveniences for women, without losing time they set out from the marketplace where the bus had dropped them, along a broad metalled road lined with buildings. Quite a few of these housed shops and offices. Two shops were selling audio and video equipment, with television sets running on the display windows and stacks of cassettes and discs near the door. Side by side were three national banks, an office complex exhibiting the government logo, and a post office. There were two doctors, a dentist, and an optician, the latter unmistakable because his wares were generously advertised at a window above which jutted out the huge model of a pair of spectacles. Where the buildings started to thin out, a sprawling compound enclosed a bungalow nestling among huge trees.

She was surprised to note that this was the police station.

The road now became an embankment, separating two sets of paddy fields with bare-bodied men at work. Looming before them was a mass of green darkness where the road seemed to reach the horizon. Somewhere in this verdure was the village which had the house of their ancestors. The dark stain grew in size and resolved itself into groves and trees, thatched cottages and people moving about. The horizon receded further, and a turn from the road showed a few brick houses. Soon they took a dirt road that forked across pasture land dotted by cows with tinkling bells around their necks. Towards the end was a broken wall that must once have surrounded the unexpectedly spacious single-storeyed house which they were now approaching.

The bricks of the arch which had framed the gateway were still intact and she felt strange as she followed her cousins through the archway, although they could just as easily have skirted or jumped over the few remaining bricks of the wall. Turning back once, just before passing under the arch, she saw through a gap in the trees of the orchards surrounding the house, fields stretching all the way to the horizon. Following her gaze, one of the cousins said, 'Our lands are out there.' But what had actually caught her eye was the statue of a man sitting on the ground with its back to the house. It was an odd posture for a statue and an odd place in which to install it.

The house itself showed signs of recent maintenance and they could make out that it had been treated to a lime wash. 'All done to impress on us the costs,' her cousins muttered to her and amongst themselves. She kept quiet, absorbing the pleasing façade of the house that had belonged to her forefathers. The house itself was built on an imposing, raised platform and as they moved towards it, youngsters from the house rushed down the steps to welcome them. A pretty girl took her arm and led her up the steps to where her aunt, an old and wizened woman, bent with age, sat on the porch on a wicker chair, gently smiling at her, while behind her, were her two cousins, hovering diffidently, shirts thrown over their usually bare torsos. They had all been living in the ancestral home, tending to the attached lands and orchards.

She touched the old woman's feet. The latter looked pleased at this simple gesture of respect. The wife of the elder of the two brothers came out swiftly through the doorway, and putting an arm around her shoulder, took her inside to the chattering welcome of the women and children of the family. She was relieved when the girl who had come down the steps to her, and whom she now recognised as the elder cousin's daughter, took her away from the melee of relatives to her mother's room, where she was supposed to stay for the night.

Daylight was soft when she came out to the terrace, where tea was being served in expensive china, brought out for the occasion. The bathroom had all the usual fittings but the taps were dry and one was expected to take water from a drum. However, there was no dearth of water and she had no problem in freshening herself up. Her aunt smiled and nodded to her to sit on the mat by her side. Then, without qualm, she immediately launched into a full-length inquisition about her life, inquiring especially about her mother, whether she had attained menopause or not and other such uncomfortably private matters.

The statue was now directly in the line of vision and she thought of asking about it, but at the last moment something prevented her from doing so.

After the sun had set below the horizon, daylight began to fail swiftly and the fields visible through the trees darkened into patches. Her eyes widened in amazement as she saw the statue rise up, turn around and walk straight through the archway, towards the house. Only then did she realise that the statue was actually a man who had been sitting motionless for so long.

Now he walked right past them in firm measured steps across the verandah, towards the door of the house, returning shortly to sit on the ground at one corner of the terrace.

The upper part of his body was bare and he wore only the doubled loin cloth, a traditional dress in this part of the country. He was tall and fair and without a single layer of the flab that middle age brings to sedentary people. He wore his hair long but not unkempt. A salt and pepper beard covered his face.

While passing her the first time, he had looked intently at her and when he returned, he looked at her again, this time with a smile. Nobody else seemed to notice him. As darkness fell, lights were turned on inside the house. She had already noticed the bulbs and the fans which were a symbol of the progress made by the village. Outside, however, the terrace remained in a restful shadow.

Next morning, a wild chatter of birds awakened her at dawn. The first rays of the sun had just begun to lighten the sky. Her sister-in-law, and the pretty niece who had slept in the same wide bed with her, were already up and could not be seen. The drum was a little less than half-full now but she could still indulge in an early bath without hesitation.

She came out to the terrace, savouring the freshness of the air. By now the sky was filled with colour, the sun had come up, a red disc brightening to dazzling yellow in a remarkably short time. The man whom she had seen yesterday as a statue was working in the garden below the terrace, sweat glistening and running in streams down his bare body. On noticing that she was looking at him, he raised a hand in acknowledgement, but did not stop his digging.

Soon, all the other cousins began to arrive, having spent the night near the railway station at the house of a relative who had actually been instrumental in the brokering of the deal. There was breakfast in an inner courtyard with everyone sitting on the floor. Happy bantering and teasing went on between sisters-in-law and nieces, even though the kitchen and the courtyard were in a flurry of activity, having to serve the large party of cousins and the numerous children of the house.

She tried to participate in the serving, but everyone protested. All said and done, she was a guest! The work for which they had all gathered, was to start right after breakfast. She noticed that though the brothers residing in the house had breakfast with them, the man who was digging in the garden didn't bother to come in.

The buyer to whom they were selling off their land was a local landowner wanting to make a foray into the lucrative business of property development. He doubled as a clerk in the land revenue office, with a bizarre anachronism for an official title. The empire had turned to dust, but the title had lived on. This title-holder was now sitting with the broker sifting through the requisite papers in an outer room attached to the terrace. The stacks of papers finalising the sale were supposed to be signed in front of the revenue officer who was also the registrar. In order to speed up the whole procedure at the time of registration, the papers had actually been signed beforehand; but the custom was that all signatories, or their authorised agents, were to attest an affidavit in person, before the officer. It was this requirement which had necessitated her journey here. Other than that, the various rounds of negotiations with the buyer and even the signing of the agreement for sale, had all taken place at the residence of her city cousins.

Breakfast upset her. Two cousins, who had arrived just that morning, spoke pointedly of the coconuts and the seasonal fruit visible in the orchard. This put the elder sister-in-law in an awkward position and she immediately sent out servants to run down to the orchard. Even before they had finished breakfast, to the intense embarrassment of the girl, luscious slices of seasonal fruit were set before them on plates and coconut water in tumblers. These cousins had been obsessed with the fact that the folks residing in the ancestral house had been enjoying all the fruits of the land to the exclusion of everyone else.

The point that the residents had for so long been enjoying sole possession of the house and lands had been brought up again and again, and every offer they had made of buying the entire house out of their share of the proceeds of the sale fell on deaf ears. Then, the girl had pointed out that only because of these very residents had it been possible to keep possession of the property intact, without any encroachment or even usurpation of any kind, which is so often the fate of the property of absentees. In fact, she had said, she was surprised that they were agreeing meekly to an equitable division, when they could have used their de facto possession as a bargaining counter for carving out a disproportionate share for themselves.

While the papers were being signed, she remained seated by the window overlooking the terrace and saw the digger as he came in, flushed with the exercise and covered in sweat. After the signing was over, they all trooped out to go to the office which was on the main street they had walked down the previous afternoon. There had been a shower the previous night and the dirt lanes across the paddy fields connecting the house to the paved way leading on to the street, had become slushy. The mud clung to her shoes. She took them off and followed the rest of the people who already had their shoes dangling in their hands. Finally, the mud was washed off at a clear puddle when they stepped onto the paved way, and everybody put on their shoes once again.

In the office itself much was made of her and she was whisked into the chamber of the officer who promptly made seating arrangements for her and, overruling her protests, ordered tea. A young woman signing for property was clearly still a rarity in these parts. Despite the warm and attentive welcome, she was soon feeling annoyed when she learnt that after a month or so, she would have to make the journey again. Today, only the sale was being finalised and they were applying for registration, along with payment of the requisite fees. The registration itself would follow in time after the application was checked and the details of the land in question, verified.

She felt drained by the time they returned and would have liked to lie alone in bed for some time, but her excited nephews and nieces had other plans. They were happy to see their city-bred aunt, breathtakingly lovely and young enough to be included in their generation, although they were also somewhat disconcerted by her self-possession and confidence. The eldest nephew, about to take his school-leaving examinations, was visibly smitten, and pestered her continually for her cell phone number. She had realised the previous evening that she should have brought little presents for them, but the ancestral lands and their occupants had been shadowy concepts to her, and her mother had not known either how many children she would find and how old each one was likely to be. This morning, she had taken care of the oversight by buying loads of sweets and chocolates and was now content to see them swarming all around her on the terrace, happily munching away. She looked out through the gap in the foliage and there he was, sitting at his post in the shade of the ancient tree where the meadow began—a statue gazing out at the seemingly endless horizon.

After lunch, at which the lady of the house had ensured that fruits had been included, she felt decidedly sleepy. But the sun was veiled by light clouds and there was a pleasant breeze. The youngsters wanted her to take a tour of the lands with them. When she tried to wriggle out of it, the elder niece laughed and said, 'You have never come to see your ancestral lands even once in all these years, and now you will just sell them off and leave without even taking a look?'

The complaint had been meant to be banter, but it was also so true that she had no excuses. Just as she was about to give in, the observer of the horizon, who'd had his meal with them, though in a separate corner of his own, came and stood beside them. He smiled at her and calling the elder niece by name said, 'Look at her. She is falling asleep in her chair. Let her rest for an hour or two, and then I too shall accompany you.'

He had a soft, firm voice, and it looked like he enjoyed a good rapport with the children because they all dispersed quietly.

The elder niece, who seemed quite contrite not to have noticed her tiredness, took her to her room to rest. However, before entering the house, she glanced back. He was moving towards the gap in the avenue, through which he would, she now knew, walk to his post.

Later, after she had rested, he showed her the lands and its myriad colours, unseen to the untrained eye, while the children chatted on, a riot of laughter, wandering through the usually still and quiet countryside. He taught her to distinguish cultivable land from pasture lands, most of the former being under paddy. And then he told her the story of the land itself.

Much of the land had been acquired by her great-grandfather from the profits of a gold jewellery business, run from a shop at the district town.

Some of it, she was a little embarrassed to note, had also been obtained through moneylending. The shop was no longer there, but its goodwill had continued to help the eldest of the brothers in the village, who had a shop in the same area. She laughed inwardly as she thought of her unforgiving cousins, who had it been possible, would have laid claim even on the goodwill.

They wandered over to the meadow where he sat regularly, and she was stunned by his tree, a veritable giant of a tree, with several subsidiary trunks going down from the main branches till it was a one-tree grove. In fact, from the house, she'd thought that there were many trees where he sat.

The meadow was dotted with grazing cattle and stretched into a collection of diverse species of trees on the opposite side. But it was the orchard which he showed around with the most pride and affection. Every tree was an individual to him with a separate history and while apprising her about it, he went on patting the trunk as if it were a horse. The orchard had been set up by her grandfather, although some of the trees were even older, having been planted by the old usurious jeweller himself.

The shadows lengthened, and it was time to leave. The broker had plans to go back to the city and had hired a station wagon. He was quite ready to take anyone along with him. She had known of the arrangement beforehand and joined in for a ride back home. They set out before sundown because the approach roads to the city were choked up during late evening. She said her farewells at the house and came out together with the same two cousins who had come with her, and two others who were planning to get down on the way.

He was standing near the solitary gate, smiling at her. She was touched by the fact that he had broken his routine to bid her goodbye. 'Come again,' he said lightly.

The entire group of excited youngsters, together with curious neighbourhood children, swelling into large numbers, accompanied her to where the car was waiting and sent her off with great gusto.

She started nodding off to sleep in the car right away and her return journey was broken into fragments of sleep, with a succession of vivid dreams: the house as it first looked from the gate, her sisters-in-law fanning the deity during evening prayers, the meadow with grazing cattle, a circle of children chanting 'She will sell off and run away,' the ringing laughter of the eldest niece on being asked about boyfriends and, again and again, overpoweringly a tree which was many, and a statue which stood up and smiled to say, 'Come again.'

As they approached the city of their destination, her cell phone rang. It was her suitor, a colleague from the office, whom her mother wanted her to marry. Though usually she didn't dislike thc attention he showered on her, this time she was disturbed because the untimely call had jangled her half-asleep nerves. She responded angrily to all his questions and the call ended rather soon. As the massive bridge they were passing over vibrated under them, the present absorbed her and her visit quickly dissolved into shadows at the back of her mind. Then her phone rang again. This time it was her mother, anxious to know where she was. She looked into the distance.

Where was she?

A brief spell of rain had left the roads glistening under the streetlights.

THE MAN WHO SAW COLOURS

Her mother was at a loss when she first described the man whom she had mistaken for a statue. Then suddenly, the unhappy times the older woman had spent in the inhospitable house, the house that she thought she had put behind her for good, caught up with her and a host of memories flooded her mind. Through the labyrinth of remembrances, a quiet face with brooding eyes came to the foreground, and she exclaimed, 'Oh, you are talking about the stepson!'

It had so happened that the crafty old moneylender had, in his declining years, fallen for the daughter of a penniless tenant. She was a pale, insignificant looking girl, with a pretty face. He married her in the face of understandably intense opposition from his wife of fifty years—a formidable woman, in whose quiet, tyrannical running of the household even he dared not interfere. He also had a grown-up son—already married and blessed with children—who resented his father's remarriage.

The young wife was mercilessly ill-treated by her senior in a thousand unobtrusive ways and soon died, leaving behind a son. It was a quirk of fate that the old matriarch took the motherless infant to her bosom and, with fierce possessiveness, brought him up just like her own grandsons.

She shooed her husband away whenever he came near him, complaining to the skies that the old devil had killed the poor innocent mother (her hostility towards the other woman having surprisingly vanished and now she too was referred to as a victim) and given half a chance would kill the poor boy as well. She would, no doubt, have spoilt him irrevocably had she lived, but the elderly couple passed away soon after the boy began to walk and talk. His half-brother's wife was a good soul and he grew up without special attention, but also without any marked neglect.

He grew up to be a hardworking farmer, quiet and taciturn, his only expression of insecurity being an excessive interest in gods and goddesses. At every village fair, he bought idols and earthen images and placed them in alcoves on the top of the doors of the various rooms. He had no confidante or special friend and no one knew what went on in his mind. The first outburst, which indicated some problem, took place shortly after his twenty-first birthday.

His brother's wife would get up at the crack of dawn, take a bath and perform her ritual prayers at the temple—actually a room housing the image of the family deity, a statue carved out of an alloy of eight metals. As the statue was valuable, the temple room was locked up at night, but the family members and older servants knew the nook where the key was concealed.

One morning, as the mistress of the house walked towards the temple room after her bath, she saw that the door was already open. Taking it as another sign of the declining faculties of her aging husband—his task being locking the house up at night—and making a mental note of remembering to have this duty transferred to her son, she went in serenely. To her horror, the idol was missing. In the hue and cry that was raised, and during the search of the premises, it was found that each little niche housing an idol gaped emptily. The mistress, who was the only one who could or cared to understand the thought processes of the collector of idols, approached him where he was sitting on the platform looking out to the land beyond.

On being asked about the mystery, he calmly replied, 'I have thrown them all into the water.'

Thus began the tedious process of fishing nets being cast into the pond to retrieve the idols. The eight-metal statue and the larger statuettes made of stone, were recovered. The earthen idols, however, had been disfigured irrevocably by the water.

The family priest re-installed the guardian deity in the temple room with the appropriate incantations and ceremonies, and also placed the smaller idols there. When the perpetrator of the crime was questioned by his much older half-brother, he maintained a studied silence. When he was goaded on, he began to display signs of excitement. The mistress of the house had to step in to stop the inquisition which, by then, had become quite a spectacle in front of the family and curious servants. He marched off to his sister-in-law and whispered, 'They are of no use.'

She was a clever woman and even though she had been taken aback, she thought it better to solve it amicably. She told him that sometimes she felt the same about them, but even so, he was not to inconvenience those who thought them to be of use.

He thought for a while and then agreed to her proposition. It would be okay to have the idols back and those who clung to their faith could go ahead and do their prayers.

'So, there won't be a repetition of today's act?'

He shook his head.

For some time after this, he remained a recluse. He wouldn't shave, washed minimally, ate little, and slept for only an hour or two at dawn. Children saw his unkempt hair and shrank away. This mood passed off after a few months and then he fell back into the routine she had seen him following.

'Didn't people try to find out what had really happened?'

'He never talked about the incident again. Shortly afterwards, your grandfather and grandmother passed away, one after the other.'

She stared pensively into the rigid skyline of the city and wondered what he thought about all day as he stared into the horizon bounding the field before him. Her reverie was broken by her mother asking her to return the phone call of the suitor.

'You should have called earlier,' complained her mother.

'Don't be ridiculous, Mother,' she replied irritably. 'My cell phone wouldn't catch signals there because there is no transmission tower nearby. Otherwise, I would have called you.'

Her mother went on grumbling but her resolute silence finally won and they went off to sleep talking about the family and the deal which would allow them to repair and refurnish their house and change the leaky plumbing and scotch-taped electrical wiring.

Next morning she was ready for her friend, but he showed up much later, just as she was leaving for work. He was a rock music buff, and while accompanying her to the stairway to the underground, he went on chattering about a concert he had attended the previous evening. She liked talking to him. They had similar interests, and she wished he was always like this. However, he spoilt it all just before she stepped down, by asking her to tea in his room in the evening, an invitation which carried the connotation of all that she had grown to reject. She shook her head and averted her glance, but not before she had seen a flash of disappointment wipe out the flushed brightness of the previous moment from his eyes. With a sigh she went down to catch her train.

As she stepped onto the sidewalk, her spirits lifted. She could feel the energy of smartly dressed men and women, all bustling to work. The boy who opened the shutters of the tiny confectionery shop, wedged in next to the entrance of the high-rise building which housed her workplace on its fifth floor, gave her a saucy grin. The lift attendant gave her a wide appreciative smile. As she pushed open tall glass doors, she noticed bright faces all around, and chattering away, suddenly, she felt a momentary return of the happiness she had known as a child.

Even the suitor, standing midway and holding a well-rehearsed pose of feigned disinterest, appeared merely ridiculous, instead of exasperating. She acknowledged him as she entered her office, which turned out to be a mistake, for as soon as she was settled in her cubicle and had lifted the first file of the day, he poked his head in and asked her to join him for lunch at the cafeteria, a simple request which would gain in seriousness if refused. Resigned, she nodded in acceptance.

The suitor was, actually, quite presentable. He was soft-spoken and polite and nobody could imagine that he was in fact, a scion of the major partner in the business. Quite unlike his elder brother, he had borne the brunt of his father's rage because of his very gentleness. His flair for painting had been ridiculed and he had been relegated to the position of a junior clerk here for not being aggressive enough. On his part, he was perennially apologetic about his father's and elder brother's behaviour in the office.

Even now while they ate, he was explaining to her why he could not attend art school.

'My father, you see,' he spoke earnestly, 'is a Philistine,' and he was not speaking pejoratively. His only concern seemed to be that she should understand, exactly, his father's attitude. The men in the office were protective towards him and the girls thought him sweet. He was loved by everybody like a kid brother. She could never make her mother understand that in spite of the presence of undeniable affection, you don't marry the likes of your kid brother! Her mother was interested in the match, not only because he was his father's son, but also because she sensed that behind his seemingly insignificant personality, he was responsible and fair, which, along with loyalty, she prized as essential foundations for a lasting marriage. Having successfully brought the meal to an end, just as he seemed to be preparing to bare his soul, she jumped up and began walking briskly towards the cash counter. He rushed to overtake her at the counter to pick up the tab, and another session was over. Her mother had enlisted the help of the uncle next door. She had called him to have tea with them on a few occasions when the suitor was also present. Having sized up the subject, he had open talks with her.

'Don't you like him?'

'Of course, I do! Otherwise, why on earth would he be here?'

'Then, why do you reject his proposal?'

What she really wanted to say was that it was none of his business. What she ended up saying was, 'Uncle, marriage is an entirely different thing altogether!' Then with her head held down and after an awkward pause, she explained, 'I get bored with him easily. The thought of his company for twenty-four hours a day, seven days a week, is difficult to imagine for me.'

However, her arguments seemed to have no leeway with him, 'Look, he paints. Surely, he must have some ideas in his head?'

'Well, if he was really passionate about art, he wouldn't have meekly submitted to his father's demands.'

Each time, these exchanges ended exactly where they started, and tired her out as she went through the familiar rigmarole.

~

This time she had pooled in resources with her two city cousins to rent a car for the day. Their nearest cousin from the suburbs would also join them on the way. The car was to reach the cousins first.

She woke up early to see her mother already up and about, packing lunch for her and preparing dry snacks to share with everybody during the journey. She gave her an affectionate hug for her efforts, bathed quickly, had a cup of tea and ran out into a clear morning to join her cousins in the journey. The car did not follow the main highway like the bus, but sped along bumpy byroads. What they suffered in terms of discomfort, they gained in terms of time. They reached the house before noon. Looking back over her shoulders as they passed through the gate, a warm glow of satisfaction suffused her when she saw the statue motionless under the tree. The family gathered around her once again and after she had extricated herself from the excitement and chatter, and had greeted her aunt, she learnt from the resident cousins that the buyer had sent word that the registrar would be a little late. They were to go to the office after lunch. Like last time, there would not be any payment, and so the business of the day would not take up much time. Everyone else arrived shortly.

Plates of fruit and homemade sweetmeats were placed before them after they had freshened themselves up.

Unable to contain herself, she promptly rose with her plate and sought permission to go out to the tree under which sat the 'Step-greatuncle'. A few eyebrows were raised at this, but nobody objected. Her aunt insisted that the eldest niece should also accompany her.

'So, how has your school been?' she asked her young niece affectionately.

'The usual. Not very interesting,' she replied with a sigh.

'What would you rather do?' she asked and saw her niece's eyes light up with a smile.

'You're the only one whom I can tell that I'd love to be a fashion designer. To design dresses for people around me ...' she went on for a while chatting animatedly. She told her that the tailor at the market had been impressed by the cuts and designs she had shown him and had offered her work to take home for the holidays. But this had met with strong disapproval from the family, and a serious threat from her father that if it continued, he would be forced to start looking for a match for her.

They walked hand in hand, the younger drawing comfort and strength from the other.

He turned around at the sound of their approach and looked genuinely pleased to see her. There were polished stones under the tree and he waved to them to sit down.

'So, you have come for the signing,' he said. It was a question as well as a statement, and she was mildly surprised to note his awareness of the world around him.

'Yes,' she said and sat for some time in contented silence, gazing out to the meadow and beyond, to the horizon, trying to see what he saw there hour after hour, day after day.

Finally she asked, 'Last time I came and saw you sitting here and looking. What is it that you see?'

He looked at the eldest niece and then back at her, his eyes knotted in thought. The frown slowly left his face as he began to answer her question.

'The colours,' he said in a low voice, 'so many of them together, merging and separating, trembling in a haze as the sun rises.'

Then he stopped and searched her eyes, 'Do you see them?'

She saw the steel grey sky above, pale blue near the horizon, white clouds and green grass and foliage serenely beautiful. But they were all parts of a still picture, not alive as he saw them, colours within outlines of shapes, not existing independent of objects, neither flowing nor shimmering, as they presented themselves to him.

But he was already describing what he saw, 'Mango leaves are bright green clusters on a deep green background. The green of the tamarind is different, fresh and airy. Lime leaves are dark and succulent. I see the greens and I know the leaves are there, but I don't see them. Leaves are not always green. You know this. Mango leaves turn red. Red on green is a sight to remember. Death for most leaves is brown coloured and when mango leaves begin to turn brown, one knows their time has come.'

His discourse was about the world, but strangely, it was not the world they saw; it was a world within another world and he peeled off layer by layer as he talked. Even her niece fell under the spell of this abstraction and stoppedfidgeting, her initial impatience giving way to a sense of wonder and peace.

He continued: 'The colours change with light. They are deep and dark before sunrise, the leaves barely distinguishable from the stems, darkness against a barely lighter background. Then the stars fade away, as light washes the sky with grey and rose till the sun rises—a huge red ball. Then colours flow down the meadow and the trees as the sky pales through progressively lighter shades of blue, the tints and hues on the land changing all the time, till the gold spreading from over the sun contracts it to a yellow dazzling disc. In the evening again the same orchestra of colours is played, this time in pastels, blue deepening to indigo from the horizon upwards, flecked by clouds with red and orange underbellies, shading into a velvety crimson; the sky draining the very colours it gave to the trees and the meadow, darkening till a silver moon rises if it does, and a haze of electric blue covers all.'

After stopping and looking at them for a moment he continued, 'I see all this every day, but the colours are never the same from one day to the next. Even the clouds, are never the same. The dance of the trees and the trembling of leaves in the wind never repeats itself. The colour of the young leaves of spring deepens through the summer. The rains darken the shade and then yellow flecks appear. Some get discoloured rapidly and fall before winter arrives. Those that survive, turn yellow in winter, then brown under the gaze of the sun and drop; their life over, just as naturally as it had started.'

Tears filled her eyes.

The afternoon stillness hovered like a sentient presence. He sighed and went on, 'If you clear your mind and learn to listen, you will also hear the sounds. Brown ants and weevils and earwigs bustling below the rotting leaves, red ants scurrying under the bark, in the background, all of which you will hear only when the birds suddenly fall silent. Otherwise, the chirping of crickets is what you will hear most of the time. At first, you will hear a constant whirr and then, as you learn to listen, you will catch the variations from morning to night, and finally, from moment to moment.

'In the evenings you will hear the wild chatter of birds coming home and nothing else. Soon, their talk drowns all other sounds till night shuts them up and then the sounds of the night take over.

'Sometimes, a bird breaks into song early in the morning. But those that sing, do it best in the afternoons. The most interesting calls are also reserved for this time of the day. When the midday first starts becoming warm after the winters, you will hear the cuckoo's call, although I have heard one clearly at midnight too. In summers, you will hear the keening of the hawk, faint because of the height, but sharp, incisive, cutting down through the afternoon air like a tiny bolt ...'

Who knows how long he would have gone on, but the niece had kept an eye on the house and saw her mother the moment she emerged on the verandah, calling them back. She rose and the spell broke.

'Go, little cousin, you must be hungry,' he said.

'I have never heard him talk so much and for such a long time,' the niece told her as they walked back towards the house.

The dinner and then the signing of the deeds, the hustle-bustle at the office, the brief shower, which delayed them and forced her to take tea under the openly admiring gaze of the registrar, the careful walk back over muddy pathways—all appeared like a dream to her, a part of an unreal, childish charade that is played in all seriousness by grown up men and women. She smiled absentmindedly as she thought of the inanities of life, drawing puzzled glances from her relatives. They were having tea before departing and while all the others were in high spirits at the conclusion of the sale, and were setting a date for a final, grand get-together feast, she wondered whether the stepson would come to see her off. Again, a certain warmth stole over her when she saw the statue rise and the man move towards the house with a purposeful stride.

She sauntered to the edge of the terrace to meet him, and before he could say anything, shouted out, 'There will be a feast and we will come back next month,' and was rewarded by the radiance in his eyes. She sank into a corner at the rear of the car, her mind returning to the tree and the meadow. It was then that the thought struck her like a physical blow: the sale was over, the tree and the meadow no longer theirs, both now belonged to the buyer, a property developer. What would happen to the meadow? Would the tree be cut down? Where would he sit and what would he see? She felt herself overwhelmed by a huge wave of guilt. Did he know what was going to happen?

~

The suitor had been invited to tea mainly at the insistence of her mother. He was asking about her last visit to the village, in great detail. She hesitated to speak of the man who saw colours. She had told her friend and had been disappointed with his response. He had always been disapproving of her male acquaintances and took them as threats. The fact that the man was not a possible rival was clear to him, but he was upset by the depth of the impression he had made on her. In the absence of any philosophy for himself, the man's talk about colours sounded like the nonsense of a madman to him.

So, she steered clear of any further argument. But the suitor remained his usual diffident and quiet self while she told him all that the man said and did. He heard everything in absolute silence and then made quite an unexpected remark.

He said that Van Gogh had an astigmatic vision, and the world was blurred to him. Some art experts have ried to say that a point of light was a blob to him. This had led to the characteristic blurring of contours and the representation by colours without outlines, observed in his paintings.

'I think your relative suffers from a similar defect of vision,' he announced prosaically.

'Trust him to wash off all the romance from any circumstance, however out of the ordinary,' she thought. But she could not just laugh it away, for she knew that such a benign defect would have remained undetected in that household. Nobody cared, and he himself would just have accepted it as a condition of life and adapted to it.

This is as much thinking as she could indulge in, for, suddenly, her friend arrived. After they'd had tea, the three young people went to her room. Soon the friend grew aggressive towards the suitor, interrupting him, and making pointed remarks about people who never understood when they had overstayed their welcome. The suitor, who had encountered such hostility earlier also, did not rise to the bait at first. He even withstood comments about his appearance and abilities. While she watched helplessly, things turned worse when he began touching her to prove his claim. After a few minutes of acute embarrassment, the suitor left. Her friend followed her back to the room, excited at the prospect of a quarrel, because that always meant reconciliation, which often paved the way for him to force himself upon her. However, this time she remained calm, and this disconcerted him. 'I want to rest,' she said and closed the door on him. Then all the the pent-up emotions surfaced and she threw herself on her bed and cried into the pillow.

She had to regain her freedom. 'What a fool I was to have lost it in the first place,' she thought.

THE GIFT

It had been decided that all progeny of her father's clan, would be invited to the final feast. Her mother would also be going with her. This had encouraged her aunt, the mother of the two city cousins, to join in.

This time they made an early start. Her mother was on medication, which required her to watch her fluid intake to avoid dehydration. She had packed adequate water and fruit juices apart from the sandwiches her mother had made for everyone. But age, the constant enemy, was against the older women, and midway through the journey, they complained of cramps in their legs. The car had to be stopped thrice to let them stretch their legs and sip juice. But it had been long since either had journeyed so far and their enthusiasm for it overruled bodily discomfort. They arrived at the house in high spirits.

Both had been newly weds here decades ago, till their husbands had left for the big city. This was their first visit since then, bringing back a host of memories. They spoke continuously on the way and towards the end she fell asleep, her head resting on her mother's shoulder. She made a pretty picture and her aunt whispered to her mother, 'How I wish she had been mine.' When she next opened her eyes, they were churning up dust on the way to the house.

Then making sure that the familiar figure was at his post, she directed her attention to the reception of her mother by the families of the house. Her aunt was an orthodox widow, who wore a white borderless sari and ate strictly vegetarian meals. But she and their neighbours had forced her mother not to indulge in either of these abstentions. Her mother wore whatever colours and prints she wanted to and ate with her daughter.

At first, family gatherings were a problem—widows were served separately and so people were confused as to where they were to be seated. Doubtful glances were not a rarity either, and, for a while, her mother stopped going to marriages and other social ceremonies. Though she never spoke about it but there must have been some snide remarks too within the school where she taught. Time bred acceptance. More and more women from her mother's generation spilt out of professions like school-teaching and nursing, where the presence of women had been accepted for long, to invade male preserves in business establishments, banks, courts and doctor's chambers. But, she had been worried about her mother's first appearance as a widow in this backwater.

To her relief, she found that there were no startled looks or pursed lips at her entry. Either the families here knew everything already from the grapevine and had decided to accept with grace things over which they had no control, or they were well-bred and good-natured enough to conceal any surprise they might have felt. What she saw, in fact, was the three wives holding hands and in tears; memories of their long dead husbands, companions of the youth they had spent here, rising like the vapours of a mist from the stones of the house which had borne them and had raised them to manhood. The strange mystery surrounding siblings reached out across the spent decades to fill her with awe, and assailed her with a ghostly residue of feelings which she had never known first hand. Then her niece came and took her hand and peals of laughter from the children brought them all back to the present.

Her previous visits had made her sisters-in-law and nieces familiar with her and she had no difficulty in making them waive the formalities of welcome, allowing her to start off for the meadow immediately after she had freshened up. She had a plan which required quick action before the lazy noon-break fell like a cloak on all activity here.

She stopped short behind the man and although she had tried to be as soundless as possible, he sensed her presence and turned to her with that same smile, which she had grown to regard as her real welcome to the house of their fathers. She got to the point immediately and spread out the day's newspaper, which she had brought from home, on the ground in front of him.

'Read it,' she commanded.

Obediently, he read out the headlines and then, confirming the suspicions of the suitor, began to falter more and more as the print grew finer. He had to bring the sheet closer and closer to his eyes.

'You are going to get a pair of glasses,' she announced. He pondered over her statement and she watched in eager anticipation as to how he would react. He sighed as if resigned to it and said, 'It cannot do any harm.' She let out a whoop of joy and pulled him up by the arm. The two started off for the house. Her sisters-in-law were taken aback by the reason for the stepson's change into outdoor clothes, but the mistress of the house, her aunt, gave her seal of approval by expressing the same opinion as the man himself. 'It cannot do any harm,' she said, 'provided he doesn't break them and cut himself.' She went on to elaborate, to her two sisters-in-law darkly, 'I once knew someone who blinded himself with his glasses.' 'These will be unbreakable, not really made of glass,' she explained. Her cousins were doubtful whether the optician in their small marketplace would have such lenses.

His outdoor dress was also robe-like and with his finely-chiselled features, salt and pepper beard, and russet mane of hair, he looked as distinguished as a Roman senator to her, and she couldn't help thinking that he must have been a handsome man in his youth. The optician, they soon found out, stocked all the latest materials and designs. She was helped by the shop owner who was keen on selling a pair of expensive unbreakable lenses which did not find ready buyers in this community of thrifty farmers. The man, she found out had acute myopia and a substantial astigmatism, the latter blurring his vision at all distances. The suitor had been right! His age had also affected his near vision. He would need a set of reading glasses too.

'Two pairs would be needed by the gentleman,' the shop owner gleefully declared. 'My technician can't make up bifocal lenses in such a short time.'

'But I don't read,' he interjected.

'Not even the newspapers?' she asked.

'I used to read the daily paper, but I didn't like the news,' he replied diffidently.

'But won't you read the letters I shall write to you?'

'You will write to me?' he asked with a happy glow on his face as she nodded. Then she was sad because she knew it was unlikely that she would come here again.

The man took child-like pleasure in choosing a frame, looking again and again at his face from different angles in the triple mirrors handed to him. But she didn't agree with his choice and he readily accepted the frame pointed out by her. The shop owner, of course, knew all about him and, for that matter, all about her as well. They went home after she had made the payments. He promised to send the glasses over later in the afternoon to the House with the Gate. While returning, he was in an uncharacteristically agitated mood. When the gate of the house was in sight, he blurted out, 'I do have money, you know.'

'Yes I know,' she responded, 'But I want you to have something from me, which will not allow you to forget me at any time.'

He laughed, 'It matters to you whether people remember you or not?'

'Of course it does! Won't it matter to you if I don't remember you day after day?'

He fell silent and then as they passed through the gate, he said, 'No.'

A look of pain appeared in her eyes. He took her hand in his own and said, 'But I shall not forget you.'

Her hand lay limp in his huge paw and it was only when they were on the steps to the terrace that she managed to give a little comforting squeeze to it as she withdrew her own hand.

The dinner, which was the mainstay of the day's programme, lasted for a long time. There were interminable jokes aimed at people, one arising from the other. The three elders had numerous anecdotes about the cousins and their childhood; not too complimentary at times, but greatly engaging and entertaining to the children who, having finished their meals earlier, circled about the diners. She took some time to pull away her thoughts from the man, but the light-hearted recollections of the past and the bonhomie and relaxed ambience of the present slowly drew her into the general merriment. For once, her pretty young niece was not serving and had been allowed to dine with her. She found an opportunity to whisper to the girl that in case she wanted, she could stay in their house in the city if she found a place in some school of fashion designing. The niece brightened at the thought and pressed her hand joyfully. However, soon she noticed that her eyes had clouded over with thought. Perhaps she was thinking about the formidable struggle which lay ahead in terms of convincing her parents.

The stepson ate separately, as was the rule and said nothing, though he couldn't have helped hearing everything. He finished long before they did, and when she finally came out, she saw the technician from the optician's shop fitting him with his glasses.

He waved away the man who was fussing about, trying to make him read something, and then taking the glasses in one hand, beckoned her to accompany him. He put on the glasses for distant vision after he sat down under the tree and, for a long time, kept staring at the meadow. She sat next to him, apprehensive at what might happen, now that his view of the world was changing radically. Finally, he turned and looked at her.

'I can see you more clearly, too.'

'What about the meadow?' she asked.

'Yes, I can see each individual leaf with each and every curl, turn and serration. The world is sharp, and not only are there colours but shapes, forms and outlines as well.'

'Is it still beautiful?' she asked fearfully.

'O my dear, even more beautiful!' he said effusively. Look at this tree. No two leaves are the same. The trees lining the meadow, their trunks and branches standing against the sky, the stems and leaves swaying gently in the wind, the weird shapes made by the clouds, I could see none of this earlier.'

'And the colours, are they still there?'

'Yes, yes, I can make out shades I never imagined existed. The smallest change, each nuance of tint and hue will now be revealed to me as it emerges or fades.' Precious radiance filled his face. 'You've presented me with a whole new world.'

Tears brimmed in her eyes.

He looked gravely into them.

'If you look, *you* will also see.'

'What, television antennae?' she said.

He was surprised at her response, and said, 'You will see that everywhere all is made of colour and sound,' and after a pause added, 'and form. Also, that beauty changes with time.'

'But your world is lonesome. There are no people.'

He meditated on her comment for a time. Finally, he nodded, 'I am not good with people.' His face darkened as he added, 'They look only at themselves in the mirror and like to hear only their own voices.' She realised she was probing his vulnerability and promptly changed the subject and began chatting about inconsequential facets of city life.

And then her voice broke.

'We have sold away all this. What will you do, what will you see?'

'But the orchards remain, I understand,' he looked enquiringly at her.

She nodded.

'Then I shall sit in them.'

He gazed at his new world for some time, and asked, 'How long will you stay this time?'

'We start at sundown.'

'Then we will visit the farther end of the orchard at sundown. It will hardly take a few minutes.' She acquiesced and the two of them sat looking at the forms and colours, the latter now changing fast as the shadows of the trees lengthened on the meadow.

When the meadow was fully enveloped in shadow, he rose and they walked into the orchards, waving reassuringly at the rest of the people who had gathered on the terrace for the farewells.

They were walking towards an arbour formed by a canopy of overhanging branches and leaves. The sound made by the birds grew louder and louder as they neared it and when they were enclosed under the natural canopy, the sound took on a three-dimensional quality. It was as if the conversations of numerous birds had formed an all-pervading, yet pulsating fog of sound. The loudness assailed the mind, making normal thought impossible, holding attention imprisoned in the furious conference. She found that her mind was being drained of all consciousness, monopolised by the not unpleasant pulsing of shrill talk, like the unending clatter of a machine gun. She was drifting into another world where her friend and the suitor, her disappointments and her ambitions, her dream of becoming an author, were fast receding into puny elements of little importance. She rose and turned about. Her hold on her world was beginning to slip, and she fought back to keep her grip. Slowly, as she walked away from the cocoon of sound, the profound emptiness which had been long gripping her soul seemed to ebb away.

They came out of the orchards to find the whole group of travellers nearing the gate. She ran up the terrace to bid goodbye to her aunt. Everyone else, she noticed, was moving together with the departing guests. The stepson was outside the gate, standing a little away from the others, as always, the glasses gleaming on his face in the last light.

When she turned her head at the point from where the gate went out of view, she saw him, still gazing at her across the empty space between them.

Then, in a flurry, they got into the rented van and left. She looked back to see a huge cloud overhead in the darkening sky. A wave of tiredness assailed her and she sank back against her mother.

What he had gifted her was a secret world. At first, she kept it shut tightly within herself, daring only to peep in from time to time, because she could never stay there indefinitely. The emptying of the mind, with the draining away of all questions of worth and meaning and purpose from life, made her uneasy. It was almost frightening, and then she always had so much to do.

When the news of his death came, she was afraid that his gift too would disappear. But it was neither a thing which could decay nor a thought whose memory could fade. It would always be there, another world, waiting for her; only she was never quite ready for it. But secretly she enjoyed a detachment and calm, just knowing it was there: a madman's world, but as real and as tangible as the daily whirlwind of life around her.

THE PASSAGE OF SHADOWS

THE COMING

It was the boy who found him in the shallows. He had brought the goats to feed on the high meadow and, as usual, left them to their own devices as he climbed down the steep and unstable slopes to the sands by the river. Actually, this was quite dangerous, for the river had come closer to the hamlet only recently and the slopes were still young, and crumbled easily. The sands had formed a small oval, too small to attract developers on the lookout for property with tourist potential. The oval was bound on one side by sturdy thorny bushes with pointed, dark green leaves. The rolling of the sands down to the river was deceptively slow, the water rapidly gaining depth away from the shore. On this side, however, the ground was harder, resisting the flow of the river and creating the shallows. The bushes and undergrowth had, in fact, intruded into the water, giving rise almost to a swamp. On the other side of the tiny plaza of sand, there were sheer cliffs and no bushes. The gently bobbing fishermen's boats marked the only narrow navigable channel away from the shore.

The boy saw a smudge of white amongst the greens and decided to explore. A remnant of a man's clothing had trapped his head and was caught in the bushes. So, his head was out of the river but his body was not even visible; it was presumably underwater. The boy tried to reach him, but the thorny bushes were in the way. There was an alternate approach from the river, but the boy was afraid that the head would be pulled into water. Finally, he clambered up the slope and ran across the meadow towards the far off trees which sheltered the hamlet, forgetting all about the goats. He was so out of breath when he fell down at the shop that all he could do was to point towards the river and roll his eyes and bob his head in a pantomime of urgency.

His clothes were in tatters and when they pulled him out he was quite naked, a fair body, with deep gashes on his back and sides and an ugly wound at the back of his head. The bleeding had long stopped, but the gashes remained. The wound behind his head was black and matted, with his hair stuck to it. The whole village had turned out to watch. Never, since the boy's mother had swung herself from the garret of her house, had there been such excitement. One of the rescuers was an assistant at the nearby health centre, and he had the body turned over to start half-hearted manoeuvres of resuscitation. To everyone's surprise, within a few minutes, the man moved convulsively and began to cough up water. Breathing began. When they turned him onto his back, however, the eyes remained closed and there was a certain laxity in his muscles. It was clear that he was only just alive. Amongst themselves they decided that his appearance was another small consequence of the ongoing troubles in the land. Taking him to the hospital would only draw attention towards him. It might even be a death sentence for him, because those who were responsible for his present condition would no doubt send emissaries to finish what they had begun.

The boy's face lit up when the man began breathing again. His grandfather, the old shopkeeper, noticed this. 'Take him to the temple porch,' he instructed, when the people of the village turned to him for an answer perplexed by a situation they had never encountered before. Although the boy entreated him with pleading eyes, the old man knew that taking the man into his house would be long remembered, and retribution would not be an improbable outcome.

By the time the man had been shifted, the boy had brought a mattress of bamboo and rope, an earthen pitcher and a spoon, as well as sheets and covers. He squatted silently on the stone floor of the porch near the man's head, lightly forcing a little water at a time into the man's mouth, remaining at his post long after everyone had gone back to the day's work. He left only to have his meal with the old man and later help him shut the shop. He brought some milk too and, from the priest, the oil lamp which was always lit in the porch when there was a ceremony. Some dogs were sniffing around the porch, and he refused to come back home, when the old man came for him late in the evening. He feared what the dogs might do, but this was not the only reason why he wanted to stay. He was afraid that he would come back in the morning and see no one on the porch.

It was summer and the old man finally relented, all along shaking his head at the boy's obstinacy which had taken him by surprise. He had been a mild-tempered boy so far and was, more often than not, easily subdued. The old man went away muttering, 'Blood always tells,' cursing his truant son-in-law under his breath, only to bring back sheets and unleavened bread for the boy. Then he sat with him; both looking thoughtfully into the moonless night as the crickets chirped, interrupted continually by the shrill whining of famished mosquitoes, until the fever came. He showed the frightened boy how to cool the man's burning temples with a moist rag and then sat on until he was pushed away homewards by the boy when he began to nod off to sleep.

The man lived.

Every morning, as the eastern sky lightened long before sunrise, the boy was awakened by the sound of anklets ringing on the feet of the women as they walked to the river to finish their ablutions before the men awoke, and to bring back water in earthen pitchers. He would turn immediately to the man on his bed, always apprehensive that the porch would suddenly be empty. This morning, he was startled to see the man's eyes open. They looked calmly at him—without surprise or fear. The boy sat up quickly. Other mornings, he would have placed a hand on the man's forehead to check the fever, but today, he did not know what to do till the man smiled at him. It was a smile which took away the lines of suffering to reveal a young face and the boy felt his heart leap with sudden joy. The man pointed to the pitcher.

News travelled quickly through the village and soon the temple porch was full of people: men and children thronging inside and the women standing outside. The man could not raise his head yet, but could speak slowly and softly, one or two words at a time. The old man was talking to him. His replies were inaudible to all but those nearest to him, but everyone shifted about, craning their heads and necks to see his lips move. They felt strangely proprietorial about him, now that they knew they had saved him. The gist of his replies was passed around like a game of Chinese whispers, till everybody understood that he was actually speaking their own dialect, albeit with a city twang.

Though he said nothing about himself apart from how he felt, people could tell that he was educated. Then when he fell asleep in the middle of an answer, they realised how weak he must have become and began to disperse. As they walked away, someone referred to him as 'our visitor', and the tag stuck. He was their visitor, a guest—uninvited but not unwelcome. They felt a power over him and a kinship, because he would have died had they not intervened and, therefore, did not feel that instinctive fear and hostility which a stranger always invoked in their hearts and minds.

The boy saw all this with jealous eyes, and a certain anxiety left his face only when he found out that no one had laid any further claims on the man. It had been their tacit understanding that the present arrangement, which gave him sole guardianship, would continue, at least for the time being. When they all left, he kept watch until the man awoke briefly to take a drink from the pitcher and smiled at him again. Then he drifted away immediately and had to be woken up so that he could drink the hot broth which the old man had specially prepared as a part of his convalescent diet. The fever did not return and the old man overruled the boy's wish to stay on again that night. But he allowed a night lamp beside the man with the wick turned low.

The boy was an observer by nature and had, over the years, set up vantage points from where he could look out all over and around the village. He slept in a loft above the shop which had a glass windowpane pointed towards the temple, and there was one position in the loft from where one could look into the porch through a gap in the bamboo grove between the shop and the temple. He angled his bed so that he could just see the man's body silhouetted against the faint light of the lamp. Actually, the light and shade camouflaged objects in such a way on the porch that the boy could sense the man only when he moved. He waited patiently till this happened and then dozed off, only to wake up with a start after an hour, and wait again in panic with a beating heart, till another little movement on the porch reassured him back to sleep.

The visitor recovered gradually. He wore his hair long and let the beard flourish. This was satisfactory for all because time and again, wandering monks came and stayed at the temple with their robes of saffron or red and knotted hair and beard—prerequisites of their acceptance by householders. The people hoped he would be regarded as yet another such mendicant. He said nothing about himself or how he had come to be in the condition in which the boy found him. The villagers continued to be curious, but on the whole, respected his privacy. In any case, such wild tales had been circulating about the troubles in the land that nobody was surprised at any happenings which could even remotely be linked to them. The boy understood that safety was a concern in the visitor's reticence. Sometimes someone would ask the boy if the man had said anything to him. The boy would then stare at the interlocutor in silence until, sensing the enormity of the accusation in his stare, the inquirer would recoil in haste.

The visitor was good with his hands, slowly accumulating a little trove of borrowed tools for working on wood. The discovery of his gift came quite by accident. One of the little children who swarmed about him because he was soft-spoken and always took what they were saying quite seriously, had with her a wooden toy which hardly looked like a doll with its flat, featureless slabs for a face and body and round rods poking out of the torso for limbs. The boy was there as he always was, except when he had to go out with the goats or keep shop and cook during his grandfather's regular foraging journeys to the market town. The man asked the boy to bring a chisel and hammer from the carpenter who ran his business from a shanty beside the grandfather's shop. He worked on the doll for a long time, so long that the children felt hungry and trooped home and the boy went home to cook dinner.

When he returned with the visitor's dinner, he found him asleep. He was regaining his strength slowly and would nod off at odd hours. Beside his pallet, the boy saw the finished doll. It was exquisite, with delicate features and carefully shaped torso and limbs, with undulations on its head to suggest hair, and even indications of nails on well-proportioned fingers and toes. The girl, when she came back late in the afternoon, could not believe that it was her doll which had been so transfigured, and she looked appreciatively from the Cinderella in her hands to the little pile of shavings and slivers neatly collected and set out to be swept away. It was a sign that hard work had been done on her toy. She was happy and spread the word around. This just meant that, henceforth, he would be in perpetual demand as a doll-maker. Women also started coming to have patterns etched on their plain wooden bangles, to order miniature gods and goddesses for alcoves of worship, and to take home an unexpected gift of some exquisite figurine to be put on a shelf or hung from a wall. At first, they remained heavily veiled and spoke little. But his gentleness lifted their insecurity and as his continuing weakness brought out their protectiveness, they relaxed. On afternoons when there was a break in their daily chores, the porch would be abuzz with shy laughter and even playful banter. It was found earlier on, that the visitor had a knack of taking the stuffing out of you so unobtrusively that you would hardly notice the trap, till his smile gave him away.

Soon the boy began admonishing women who stayed too long or brought delicacies, complaining that they drained his strength with too much talk and work. His protests sometimes bordered on rudeness till a look from the man checked him and also gave him back his sense of ownership. The man was, however, also careful not to intrude into the carpenter's domain of utility items and refused to fashion shelves, chairs or stools. When the old shopkeeper suggested a rota for the supply of meals to the visitor, as was customary in the case of a monk who stayed for long, no one demurred. There was, instead, a sense of gratitude, for the village folk were extremely sensitive about dues to themselves and to others. The men did not object to the visits of the women because they regarded the visitor as their own creation; a hollow shell thrown away by the gods into which they had blown life, and not as a mere mortal, with an ever-prevailing aura of threat and danger.

Also, they were grateful for another development. The children had discovered his knowledge of figures and grammar and natural phenomena and started bringing school work to him, for elucidation and rectification. They were all first-generation learners with no one to help them at home.

Tutors were aplenty and quite cheap, but they stayed in the market town where the school was. They were well aware that no tutor would find it worth his while to journey regularly to the hamlet across the wooded hills surrounded by the river on three sides. The children brought their own little sputtering oil lamps and the porch looked like a picture from afar with tiny yellow blobs of quivering light amidst a thin haze of smoke, with the deeper darkness outside pierced only by a fluttering pattern of bluish dots formed by the fireflies.

The boy did not mind the tiny learners trailing bags too large for them, but presided over them with a stern hand. He was exasperated by the man's lack of ability to lift a hand against even the grossest misdemeanour on their part. Instead of the man's voice, which was hardly ever heard, loud admonitions delivered by the boy to his errant charges were heard frequently. Often the man had to stop his raised hand, poised to administer a tight slap to an unusually adamant miscreant.

The months which followed were among the best in the boy's life. Later, much later in life, all of a sudden, a scene from those times would flash before his eyes and he would stand rooted to a spot, staring into the distance, his throat choked with emotions welling up from the past. He would once again smell the wood smoke, as they caught the first light to start towards the hills, joyous bird song ringing all around them.

At first the man would be exhausted by the time he and the boy crossed the bamboo groves and reached the meadows on the first slopes of the hills. They would sit down on a slope, looking at the hamlet as it awoke to early morning activity, wisps of smoke rising from the huts, the long shadows quickly shortening as the light grew stronger.

As his strength slowly returned, they began to start earlier and could climb higher up the hills before he tired. By then, it would also be time for the boy to come back to his goats who would be hungry and restive, seeking grass and exercise. Then a day came when they were at the top of the hill and the countryside rolled away from them on one side. The other side, the road to the town wound its way like a thin black ribbon towards the horizon. From here, another time, they saw the hazy lights of the marketplace, with a bigger haze beside it from the district headquarters. The boy knew that the headquarters were actually much farther off, but then, distances were difficult to ascertain from the hilltop.

They went up all the hills and wound their way along the goat tracks, and soon could go from any part of the amphitheatre surrounding the hamlet to another, without ever emerging from the cover of the woods. The boy had, in the course of his lonely journeys, been into the hills before, but had never examined the woods and slopes, landmarks and their interconnections so thoroughly that they stood out in the mind as on a map. At that time, these climbs were just a part of an exhilarating exercise, but slowly he realised that there was something more to them, that there was a purpose and a plan to their excursions, but what that envisaged and tried to encompass became clear to him only later.

THE SOJOURN

The village slowly accepted the visitor as an inhabitant. Apart from the odd peddler, the only people who came regularly through the hills from the world outside were the police. Like all the neighbouring communities, the people of the village also distilled their own wine from fermented rice. This was illegal, as there was an excise duty on the manufacture of liquor, and a license for a distillery was mandatory. The police came in regularly and broke the earthen stills when they found them and confiscated packets of the fermenter. Apart from a few bottles strewn conspicuously for the police to take away for their own use, rarely did they find any other.

It was scanty booty and even after allowing for a tribute in the form of a feast in the shop with goat meat curry, where additional bottles usually materialised without comment, the police would not have come so regularly just to build up statistics to satisfy higher authorities. But the distiller at the district headquarters had an outlet at every marketplace and even in large villages, and wanted entry here. Home stills were a competition and he paid the police handsomely for discouraging cottage industry.

The people around the temple hid their bottles in a shallow bunker behind the idol's throne. This had been dug, once upon a time, by a priest of the temple to hide the ceremonial dresses of the idol and brass incense burners. At that time, the landlords, whose only mark still left in the hamlet, apart from the temple, was a ruined manor taken over by snakes, had not yet all abandoned the village. The priest was still being paid a paltry salary by the family. The bunker had a very narrow mouth, barely broad enough for pushing a hand in and retrieving bottles which could easily be concealed by a deliberate careless arrangement of leaves and twigs. The police had never found the place.

After the visitor had been given the liberty of being in the temple porch, the villagers began to hesitate about using their old hiding place. Then, one night, after the boy had left, an ill-at-ease neighbour came and sat by him. After some desultory conversation, he stood up and strolled casually to the idol's chamber. When he returned, the bulge in the waist band of his lower garment had disappeared.

There was a raid a few nights later. After their routine round, which included searching the temple precincts and a casual sign of obeisance to the visitor, who to them was just like the other holy men who stayed back as long as there were free lunches, the police left. The neighbour returned to the temple and retrieved his treasure with a smile of complicity; the visitor had passed the test, which told them he was on their side of the great divide between 'them' and 'us', and the bunker resumed its old function. The villagers came in freely to hide their bottles, at first with a sheepish glance or two at the visitor, and later as if he was not there.

As he regained health, he began to help people in their daily chores. There was insufficient land for cereal crops and rice; the staple grain had to be bought. Apart from fish from the river, there were plenty of vegetables, eggs, flesh and fowl, and also goods and services based on bamboo and wood. When the bamboo pushcart was the main method of locomotion for goods, the village had been known as a centre for making carts with wooden wheels. Now, all over the region, the pushcart had been replaced by the cycle van: a contraption made of steel tubes. It soon became the first article a man bought with his savings for going to the market with his wares. Small usurers, who kept such vans for hire, had also emerged.

The villagers fanned out into adjoining villages and marketplaces, with bamboo sticks, ropes, chopping knives, and other tools and implements. They did work as roof makers and thatchers. It was a skill which was well appreciated and well paid for. Then again, where a village boasted of its own bamboo grove, the rods and accessories were supplied to the roof maker. This was, however, a seasonal occupation, usually much in demand at the end of the rains. The earnings did not even last the year. Therefore, the womenfolk knitted bamboo baskets—large and shallow ones for carrying produce and smaller deeper ones as household bins, and various other wares.

All these could easily be taken up to the market and, during lean months, sold around the region for small profits. One or two adventurous souls had even learnt the art of tile-making and were trying to convince the little usurers to join up and set up a kiln, as bamboo and thatch were giving way to tiled roofs. Fishing was a dwindling trade as both upstream and downstream, the river was occupied by the fleets of the big traders, and there was a perennial trickle of young men from the fishing families, leaving the hamlet for the fleets.

The visitor's involvement in the daily work of the hamlet started quite by chance. He had gifted a wall hanging made from extra bamboo to a woman whose husband had the bright idea of taking it to the market. It was immediately bought off. This was reported back home and soon a delegation of the men from the village went and asked him to work for them. Thus he started fashioning wall hangings and decorative knick-knacks from leftover pieces of raw bamboo. All these found a ready market at the town among those who had just begun to store a little surplus. This, of course, turned out to be a mistake.

Late in the afternoon one day, two traders from the market town arrived in the village and sought out the vendors of the decorations. They wanted to order a special type of decoration to be sold only to them. They questioned the vendors seriously and were able to gauge by the hesitant answers of the men that the maker was elsewhere and that they were trying to preserve their exclusive selling rights. Another round of threatening and coaxing made the villagers fearful, but they still wouldn't open their mouths. Finally, a brutal threat to oust them from the market worked. Their defences crumbled and they set out for the temple with the traders.

The visitor was quick to size up the situation and in his usual soft but firm manner, made the traders understand that he was not a householder and, as such, did not need money. So, the question of dealing directly with buyers did not arise. However, he would supply through the villagers any wares that the traders specified. The traders finally gave up trying to persuade the visitor and made arrangements with the men of the village so that all wares made by him would be sold only to them for a commission. But the story of the soft-spoken, long-haired and bearded, unworldly resident of the temple in the riverside hamlet of bamboo weavers and roof makers, spread all over the region; especially because the two traders set up a shop in the marketplace, prominently displaying stuff made by him.

The community, a giant multicellular organism, could not now rest without assimilating the visitor, the first sign of which was the altered behaviour of the women they chose to giggle after a few whispers, suddenly glance at him and then dissolve into uncontrolled laughter on each other's shoulders. This was especially so for a particular group of girls in the marriageable age. Therefore, the visitor was not really surprised when one evening, one of the village elders, who bore a kinship to one of the girls of the group, decided to pay him a visit.

It was a proposal of marriage, a proposal of great honour, as the bamboo weavers were offshoots of a well-known tribe which normally forbade marriage outside its community. There must have been many closed-door meetings within the community before such a significant decision would have been taken. The visitor acknowledged the honour of the offer and pondered on how best to avoid causing offense while turning it down.

The elderly person sensed the hesitation and said, 'For a man and a woman, happiness is not in isolation but in conjunction. Your loneliness pains us and it seems that our daughter too favours you.'

'I am a wanderer,' the visitor replied, 'and such felicity is not for people like me.'

'There is a time, my son, for every wanderer to make a home for himself.' Then misunderstanding his silence, the elder changed his approach. 'Perhaps you do not understand who the daughter is? Or perhaps you do not favour her?'

'On the contrary, she is too well-favoured to throw herself away on a wanderer like me,' the visitor replied.

Not clearly grasping the meaning of these words and still misunderstanding his reluctance, the elder praised the girl, 'She is a tireless worker in the house, a fine weaver and a good cook. I'm sure you will not have any complaints...,' his voice trailed a little.

The visitor shifted his feet. This was not going to be easy. 'I'm married,' he said. The elder had clearly not been prepared for this answer. No one had thought that the visitor had any ties anywhere else. Nevertheless, he had been sent by the community for the special purpose of binding down this valuable asset of a stranger, so he went on valiantly, 'That may be the case, but how does it matter? You will be the gainer. When you visit there, you will have a wife. When you come back here, you will have a wife.' It took a long time for him to convince the elderly gentleman that his mind was quite made up in the matter. The boy was hovering just beyond sight of the elder and made a beeline for the man once he had left. Even though he could not have had an inkling of the greater issues involved, he was not happy either at the outcome: 'She's a good girl,' he advocated.

~

It was not truly light yet nor was anyone else up when the girl came. He was awake because it had been a bad night for the surviving aches and pains of his wounds.

'I asked them to make you the offer,' she said.

'I was honoured.'

'Don't talk like that! Don't you like me?'

She stood with an air of brazen defiance; unveiled in front of him, proud of the exquisite fullness of form she was offering him. She was satisfied by his look of candid admiration and then asked, 'Then why did you invent lies to avoid me?'

'What is this you are talking about?'

'You are not married. We know that.'

'How can you tell?'

'We can.'

She looked straight into his eyes, and a timeless intuition gave her sight into his tortured soul.

What she saw, he did not know.

After a while, however, she sighed and then turning her back to him, walked away with all the dignity that her beauty and youth could confer.

The villagers were disappointed, and the disappointment became tinged with apprehension when they learnt that he had asked the boy if there were any of his father's clothes left which might fit him and would not attract undue attention while travelling. Next, he asked the old man to collect some money from the men who sold his wares.

The old man asked him, 'Is it a short journey or a long one, my son, that you prepare for?' The visitor looked into the distance for a long time before he answered, 'I have to come back.' It was, in fact, an answer to the real question in the old man's mind, but some found the wordings odd when it was discussed endlessly in the village during his absence.

The boy was, however, not convinced and was distraught, hovering and circling in the background in the evenings instead of checking the excesses of the children. He was reassured somewhat, when the visitor asked him to note and remember carefully any inquiry about his journey originating from outside the hamlet. On the day of the departure, he was up and about even before the visitor awoke, and watched, from his sentinel's post, the small lamp being lit and taken from one place to another as the preparations for the journey were concluded. He came out at the right time to intercept the traveller and received a jolt at his changed appearance. Sometime in the night the barber had come and cut the traveller's hair and trimmed his beard. He felt a pang in his heart, as he realised his own exclusion from these proceedings; but soon enough, his brain put together all the happenings since the beginning of the discovery in the river, and he felt alarmed. By this time, he was almost running to keep up with the man as he glided through the darkness, and he panted out his concern. The reply wafted to him through the air, thick and heavy with impending rain and he caught only the tone which was meant to calm and pacify.

He stopped at the pass where the road to the town crossed the cleft in the hills, and, almost immediately, the rain started pouring down in torrents to shut out all view of the rapidly diminishing figure in the distance. His last words may have been something like,'Not this time,' but he could not be sure of this as he mused over the departure in his mind endlessly for the next few days.

Once again he began having nightmares, which had first started after he had found his mother swinging in the attic at the end of the rope she had herself woven from the hemp of her fields, and had only abated recently after he had adopted the visitor as his dependent. In the grisly, ashen light of his dreams, the face of his mother would fade and dissolve into the face of the visitor and he would wake up shivering in cold sweat.

All the while that the visitor was away, the boy fretted and his melancholy was intensified by the unease in the village. So far the people had found a lucky charm which gave them an identity, a recognition beyond the facelessness and namelessness of their own existence as the inhabitants of the village by the river. They had felt insecure in its absence, and found themselves not wanting to slip back into the oblivion and old ways of timeless existence.

The boy took to slipping down into the darkness after the nightmares awakened him, to check the porch in case there were no matches there or the oil had run out, though he knew that the man always kept the wherewithal necessary for a light, dry and ready.

It was the light which awakened him finally when the visitor came back. Even in his elation he paused to watch the man and was startled by a 'glint' of something in his bag. He told himself, 'He has brought gold,' but there was nothing to be seen when he came down to greet him in the middle of the night, and he promptly forgot all about it on being rewarded by a smile of welcome and genuine pleasure.

Later when he recalled the 'glint' during daytime, he searched all the hiding places he knew of, in and around the porch. They were many and he took quite a few days to account for all of them. It took longer also because he could hardly go about doing this before the very eyes of the visitor, and consequently, had to wait till the man went down to the river for his ablutions. But he drew a blank, except for the fact that one or two of the places were cleaner than they should have been after the years of disuse.

There had actually been one inquiry during the visitor's absence—a lightly camouflaged inquest under the pretence of a market survey. The villagers had not believed the motorcyclist when he spoke of collecting their 'valued opinions', because quite simply, they knew that their opinions carried no value, and told him nothing. But of course, they couldn't prevent him from going around with his clipboard pretending to find out something.

The men thought he was ogling at the girls, but the boy instantly understood that the real object of his walk through the village, right down to the river and back, was to take a good look at the porch and its emptiness.

It was evening by the time the boy reported this to the visitor. His face was in a shadow so his expressions could not be read, but the boy well knew the sudden stillness which enveloped the man's frame when he was thinking about a course of action. However, nothing happened immediately. But the boy sensed a heightening of the wariness—always present as an undercurrent. There was also a sense of relief mixed with the tension which the boy could not understand. The visitor had never spoken of the troubles so far, but now he slowly opened up to a select group of youngsters. The boy was always around when they talked and although he was never directly invited into the presence of his seniors, he was not shut out either. His rights over the visitor were well-recognised by the whole community.

The boy did not understand much of the talk but he enjoyed the stories about the visitor's adventures, though many of the stories were about troubles in far-off places, with names hard to pronounce and even harder to remember. When, later in life, he tried to gather the wisps of those memories into a tangible strand, he did not quite succeed, apart from a basic understanding that all the talk was about 'them' and 'us'. What he remembered well was the effect of these discussions on the listeners. They somehow became more soft-spoken and less impulsive in their banter. A contemplative shadow appeared in their eyes, and a certain air of growing up. These men carried the mark of the dialogues they held with the visitor all their lives and, in the years to come, the boy was to learn from them who the man was and what drove his soul.

The many sittings had coalesced into one in his memory, as such unclear occurrences often do, and all that he remembered was an afternoon in the rains.

It must have been a Sunday or a festive day for the young men to have had a free afternoon. There were three or four of them, sitting cross-legged on the floor of the porch. Water was pouring in rivulets down the gutters from the roof, and the porch was screened by curtains of rain. There were strong gusts of winds which sometimes carried droplets of cold water right to the centre of the porch where they were all sitting around a canister of tea one of them had thoughtfully brought along. The boy crouched a little distance behind the visitor after pouring tea for them into earthen cups. What he remembered was a paradox and perhaps that was why it had lodged itself into his memory for life. Someone had said, 'The main thing is that we shall become them and they shall become us.' The visitor shook his head in flat denial showing more emotion than he normally allowed himself.

'We must not become them for then nothing would have changed.'

It took the boy all his life to figure this one out and even then he was never sure that what he finally understood was indeed what the listeners were supposed to understand.

THE SHADOWS PASS

They came for him in the early hours. The lights woke up the boy, for other than that there was not a murmur. They must have left transport way out of earshot and switched on the lights when they thought they had surrounded the hamlet. The sky was lit up, but it was not a uniform glow; many beams crisscrossed and moved continuously. The boy leaped up from his bed and pausing only to put on a robe and relieve himself, ran towards the temple. The visitor had clearly been up a while, for he was already dressed and just about to put out the lamp which, as it flickered, got reflected in the oiled, shiny surface of the gun in his hand. On seeing the boy, he waved his free hand frantically, signalling him to go away. But the boy shook his head fiercely and started after him, downing quickly a few gulps of water from the pitcher to wet his mouth and throat, quite dry by now.

The streets were deserted while doors remained shut and there were no faces at windows. Every soul must have been up by now, but ancient practice told them what not to do when the king sent his men.

They waited behind closed doors and, as they stared into the darkness, imagination perhaps etched the outlines of an ascetic face and a lean, wiry form before their eyes. But they remained quiet. The idyll was over.

The visitor and the boy scaled the hills, moving freely under the mobile canopy of light because the beams came nowhere near ground level. It had been a parched summer, but the night was sultry, promising a storm and perhaps rain. The boy was short of breath for the pace was quite cruel, but he dared not pant for fear that the visitor might slow down to accommodate him or peremptorily send him back. Once they were inside the woods, the visitor slowed down and used the paths mapped out in their many excursions to reach the top in the quickest time possible. It was clear that the invaders were still on the slopes on the other side because their lights continued to throw upward beams and the trees at the top and the slopes on this side remained in shadow. Knowledge of their terrain had allowed the visitor and the boy to nullify the advantage of the invaders as first-movers.

The lights and movement had disturbed the inhabitants of the forest. Birds chirped angrily and there was a continuous flutter of wings higher up near the treetops which, of course, were lighted up. One bird with a particularly raucous voice, who rarely visited the hamlet but was known to them from their visits, this night kept up a furious barking. Squirrels kept scurrying about and insects buzzed and zoomed against their legs as twigs and dried leaves crackled beneath their feet.

While climbing up they had been hearing a whirring which increased as they progressed up the slope. When they had climbed all the way to the trees at the top, the boy's heart sank at the sight which unfolded before him. Far out on the road was a convoy of cars sitting tight. Halfway from the convoy to the first slopes was a truck carrying a massive generator creating the whirring noise. Perched high on poles fixed to the truck, was a battery of searchlights, rotating on a fan. In the blinding glare could be seen a winding line of men with guns and powerful torches attached to their helmets, as in mines, advancing up the slopes. Their advance was slowed down by the minuteness of their search, which encompassed the hills entirely.

At present the search party was only a little below the top and, taking in the scene at a glance, the visitor turned and started snaking down the shortcuts with loping steps and the boy followed. This time they were creating a ruckus and birds started flying about in small circles with furious cackles. The pursuers must have sensed this, for a growl rose from the other side. As the fugitives reached the lower slopes, the visitor asked the boy to go. An argument ensued between the two, which continued until the boy understood that it was not only for safety that he was being pushed on, but safety with a purpose. He had a task to perform, if and when the pursuers gained their objective. He wept because the visitor had mentioned 'when'. The visitor stretched out a hand but their leave-taking did not happen, for soon a roar rose as the top was flooded with light and the visitor and the boy swiftly separated to run in different directions.

But, contrary to the visitor's instructions, the boy did not run home. With tears streaming down his face, he climbed on one of his watching mounts from where he could gaze down unnoticed, right from the slopes to the river. The visitor, who was already a blur, moving just beyond the advancing wash of light, was making towards the fishermen's boats. As the boy's eyes followed his rogress, relieved at the absence of the moon, a dark mass came into view on the river and with clenched fists, nails digging into his palms, the boy watched helplessly as searchlights came to life on the gunboat. When his eyes adjusted to the glare, he saw the stretch from the temple to the river illuminated as if it were day. Only, the light was corpse blue; the visitor was nowhere to be seen.

The men from the landside fanned out, taking cover as they did so, and advanced from one shelter to another till they were roughly in an arc around the temple. Then they started firing into the temple. The staccato sounds reverberated inside the boy's head even as the advance troop rushed into the temple precincts. Two men came out and ran back to a small group behind the shop. There was hasty consultation amongst them, with some people pointing towards the silent huts and some towards the river. The latter won the argument and the lines re-formed and, still keeping cover, crept towards the boats. The boy was ashamed to feel relief. He understood well that the hamlet had just escaped vivisection.

As they came down firing from the meadow onto the sands, the visitor started firing single shots, in reply. His aim was good and there was no cover for the attackers as the gunboat had not doused its lights. Many of his shots found their mark and the sands were soon dotted with bodies. But they were far too many and their commanders were impatient. Perhaps they feared an attack from the hamlet behind them or were plain contemptuous of human life. So, instead of laying siege from the meadow or inviting a landing by dinghy from the gunboat, the charge continued. Even then they could not reach the boats till the visitor's gun against them fell silent. The boy never knew what happened in the end. Was the visitor hit or did he run out of bullets? Now, with dry eyes, he saw him being pulled out from behind the boats by his hair. A commander turned him over with his boots, took out a side arm and pumped bullets into his head. Then he turned and walked back after giving some commands with a wave of dismissal. The men carried the target and all the other bodies back with them. This time they took the main road, marching in single file with weapons on alert. But the doors still remained shut and the windows bolted. Not a sound was heard apart from the clip-clop of boots.

The boy had just enough time to enter his home before the storm broke. The old man was sitting behind the door, a ghostly presence, more so because of his unblinking stare and complete silence. The boy climbed to his perch and surprisingly, fell into a dreamless sleep. When he awoke, it was day and the air was clear.

There was the fresh scent of rain-drenched soil and joyous birdsong in the air. The dust had been washed off the leaves which shone as if freshly painted in green. All blood too had been washed away. It was as if the events of the night had not really happened.

But when the boy walked to the temple, brushing his teeth with a twig, he saw the bullet holes, the platform and a set of clothes, viciously torn to bits, the broken pitcher with a stain of water around it. Pain seized his heart in a vice-like grip but he came back to clean up. There was a silent crowd at the porch. Nobody asked the boy anything. The children were searching the ground for spent bullets.

The old man kept a sharp eye on the boy but noticed nothing alarming. There was a new detachment about him and a certain watchfulness. But his appetite, as always the prime index of his mental health, did not suffer. He developed a tendency of waking up several times at night, and his grandfather, sleepless in his old age, was able to sense each move in spite of all the precautions taken by the boy; the nightmares, however, did not recur. The old man wanted the boy to talk to him about his thoughts and preoccupations but when this failed, he cursed his son-in-law openly for having passed on another undesirable trait to his grandson.

~

She came after dusk and it was the boy who saw her first, looking like a wraith in the half light. He was tying up the goats, but as always, he had one eye on the porch. He hurried out and the old man came to the door and stood motionless on seeing the object of his haste. The boy lit the lamp which still hung in the porch. Even in the lamplight, her beauty was breathtaking. She was sitting as children do, with her arms around her legs, lips parted in inquiry, large black eyes entreating negation of what had leapt to her mind.

The boy shook his head slightly, and flinched as tears, like shiny beads, streamed down her face in the lamplight. Soundless sobs racked her slight frame so violently that the boy thought that they would break her into pieces. He had never seen such a paroxysm of grief before. As people gathered all around her, she slowly fell silent and, finally, walked down to the river to wash herself. The boy accompanied her, but she never faltered on the way. It was as if she had gone down that path every day. After the ablutions, she asked the boy to sit down. With a sign of her hands, she asked him to tell her everything. When the boy was done, she gazed out for long into the haze which was the river. But she did not weep again.

Once, she rose and walked to the boats and stood looking at the spot where he fought and fell. While returning, the boy made a detour and approaching the porch from its rear took her to the hiding place. She did not understand at first what his intention was, so good was the concealment. When the camouflage was removed she asked him to bring out the contents, but he shook his head. They were hers and hers alone. She followed his instructions and soon her hands were grasping a sealed plastic packet. She pushed it into her dress, up towards the bosom, its coldness making her shiver.

The people were perplexed about where to put her up and were relieved, although a little shamefacedly, when she opted firmly for the porch. Some of the women offered to stay with her. She held their hands, looked into their eyes and thanked them, but said she needed to be alone. They never forgot her eyes. When asked about it one day much later, the girl who had wanted to marry him said that her eyes spoke to her in spite of their sorrow and through them she felt a great peace. A hot meal was brought and the boy got with him another pitcher of water and some sheets to make a bed. He stayed with her till everybody left. She asked him about his first day of convalescence and his life in the hamlet, his daily routine, calling for details and asking again and again what his exact words were and what his expression was while saying them; when did he smile and when did he fall silent. The women had shown her some of the figurines he had made and one of these was given to her as a present by somebody. While listening to the boy, her long, slender fingers went on caressing the figurine. Slowly she fell silent and her arms dropped listlessly by her sides. The boy thought she was tired and, filling up the lamp with oil, walked back home. He ate meagrely under the disappointed gaze of the old man and retired to his perch.

She was reading what the boy thought was a letter. It was in many sheets and she read them again and again until, to the utter consternation of the boy, she began to beat her head on the floor. He wanted to run to her, but realised that it would be an intrusion. After what seemed to the boy to be hours, she fell to the floor face down and her body twitched in spasms as if she were trying to embrace the floor where he had slept, into herself and beyond. The boy kept up his watch even after she became motionless, but he must have dozed off, because he didn't hear the rooks cawing in the false dawn. When he opened his eyes, she was gone.

He went on searching for hiding places that were unknown to him. He did find some but they were mostly empty, though one or two had evidently been used; shreds of paper, broken strings, and a pencil stub. Then, in quite an unexpected place, close to the temple, he found the bundle. The sheets, when he opened the bundle, looked like the ones he had once glimpsed from afar. But they were obviously drafts. Lines had been scored out, words overwritten. He could not make much of it and realised that he needed to be educated to understand the meaning behind the words he could only spell. This was primarily the reason why he persisted, against all odds, in his quest for an education which took him away from the village and even the country. He came back to the temple only after he could understand what the visitor had written and why.

THE DRAFTS FOUND BY THE BOY

The First Sheet

When you wake up you will know
I remembered you in the night.
This passage is stark, spotted
with the wintry eyes of thin children
boring through the glass as they run barefoot on the stubble
Under ashen skies,
Unforgiving; unforgiven.

Mornings
You are a fading signal flitting through the interstices
of compulsive activity,
Useless, without purpose—a make-believe world of shadows—Card houses
to prop up failed ambitions, hollowed of hope and desire;
Abandoned ports on a receding shore.

I touch the buttons as if they are the message they can carry.
When you wake up, you will know
When night fell, I finally remembered
Your eyes as you slept.

The Second Sheet

I hesitate to think about you after nightfall
for fear you may wake up from your dream;
also it is too much pain.
As it is the heat sears me as I walk
over browned-out fields, and dried hollows, which once were lakes,
brimming with pictures of white clouds in turquoise skies, where
Now the scarred soil dies alone each day a little more,
peopled by the ghosts of these many deaths,
empty sockets, fingers poised to claw and gouge, death masks
snarling and frothing,
torn nails etching on cracked window panes
the hopeless meanderings of lost minds.

These are the pixels I cannot send.
How can I send you such thoughts?
But will tomorrow show a gleam of green in a little shadow;
a picture to attach to my mail?
I cannot tell,
and it may be too much pain even then.

The Third Sheet

Through the bars of my mind, I still look at the sky and wonder,
As the earth turns again and light seeps through the darkness
and overflows,
I wonder,
What comes to you out of the dark this day?
Can you still love, does desire still rise—
a flooding pool washing away the stains of the day?
O how ill has time used the beauty of your mind!
Thrown you carelessly aside the morning after,
An eggshell on the sidewalk,
To be trodden underfoot by many.
My dove, my little flower,
I wish you clouds to wet you whole,
and starlight for your bruised eyes.
It is just that my world is too much for me
And in the glare that is the arena
I am finally alone.
Darling, believe.

The Fourth Sheet

The storm which rides me
Where will it set me down?
And shall I still see your star then
even past the gathering darkness in the sky,
menacing and poised, clinically indifferent,
a retiarius at the kill?

It rides me hard through the habitations of the dead,
Phantom harbours and spent mines,
Abandoned sheds with broken chimneys,
The jagged, accusing digits of long dispersed queues.
Will it set me down on the pot-holed tarmac below?
Where nothing comes and nothing goes,

And shall I see your star?

... The rest was slashed out again and again. Perhaps there had been a proper letter.

ACKNOWLEDGEMENTS

I must thank Devapriya Roy right at the beginning for taking charge of this book. Without her and Saurav Jha, the book would have lived and died a manuscript. I thank Niyogi Books for the care and interest with which they have published the book and my editor, Ms Supriya Mukherjee, for her patience and effort in putting *A Triptych* together.